ORPHAN

+++++++++++++

ORPHAN

+++++++++++++

HARRY HAINES

Mayhaven Publishing

This novel does not depict any actual person or event.

Mayhaven Publishing, Inc
P O Box 557
Mahomet, IL 61853
USA

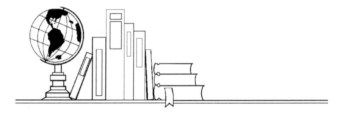

Cover Design: Steven L. Mayes
Copyright © 2008 Harry Haines
Library of Congress Control Number: 2008925661
First Edition—First Printing 2008
ISBN 13: 9781932278569
ISBN 10: 1932278567

Cover photograph, courtesy of the American Quarter Horse Association,
Amarillo, TX

To Shirley, my first reader.
(who put up with a lot to make this story possible)

CHAPTER 1

Eastbound on I-40, About 20 Miles West of Amarillo, Texas

Flashing red and blue lights warned me.

In the flatness of the Texas Panhandle—where there are no trees except those planted by hand and carefully watered—I could see the lights a mile away, and because I pulled an empty cattle trailer, I eased up on the accelerator. As the speedometer needle dropped to ever-slower numbers, another state trooper flew past me toward the accident. He pulled up near the wreckage, left his lights flashing, and ran ahead to an overturned, dilapidated pickup.

An Amarillo ambulance arrived from the opposite direction. It circled across the grass median and stopped nearby. I joined several other people who left their cars, hurrying toward the mishap. Any accident on I-40—where traffic runs at least seventy miles per hour—is almost always deadly. This one looked worse than usual, and it involved animals.

Apparently the old pickup had been pulling a horse trailer when it tangled with a yellow Porsche. Both vehicles rolled, causing the trailer to cartwheel, end over end, into an ugly heap at the side of the road. As I moved toward the debris, I heard the pitiful sounds of a mortally wounded animal—the whinny-scream of a horse in pain. A second red-and-white ambulance pulled into the area from the east, lights flashing and siren wailing.

"Driver's dead," I heard a uniformed highway patrolman say to the EMTs who approached the wrecked pickup. "The woman in the Porsche needs help." They rushed on toward the crumpled yellow car. It concerned me that no one cared enough to check on the animals. I let the others go on and stopped to see what I could do.

The wrecked horse trailer lay on its side, and from its appearance, I feared the worst. The moans of the dying animal grew weaker. I yanked open the back doors and peered inside. There were two horses—a mare and her foal.

The next few moments hammered my senses like a nightmare. The usual smell of an animal trailer came at me with an added, acrid stench of blood and internal injuries. I discovered that a steel brace, one of the main supports from the trailer's floor, had somehow pulled loose and now protruded up into the horse stall like a giant surgeon's scalpel. This three-foot knife of metal had ripped open the mare's stomach. I closed my eyes for a moment as I stood there, grimacing, and then I looked helplessly at the poor animal's intestines now spewed over the wreckage, blood everywhere. My training as a doctor of veterinary medicine wasn't needed—even a layman could see this horse was only minutes away from death.

The little colt, however, appeared unscathed. He wriggled past me, and bolted through the open door. I thought he might run away, but he didn't. Scared, he stood nearby, occasionally poking his nose into the trailer's opening to neigh softly to his mother.

A uniformed state trooper walked over. "Dr. Masterson?"

I nodded, surprised he'd called out my name. "Yes?"

"Thought I recognized you. My brother-in-law's a vet, works for Sagebrush Cattle Feeders. He's all the time talking about you and how you helped with their mad cow thing. A real hero, he says."

"Thanks," I replied, feeling a little embarrassed. I looked back at the trailer. "Right now we have a different problem."

The officer walked closer. "What've we got?"

"Two horses. The mare's dying, but this little fellow seems okay."

As we talked a shudder vibrated through the trailer. A strange sound—a sort of gasp, a release from tension—caused us both to turn toward the mare. The silence that followed conveyed an unmistakable end of life.

The foal moved closer to me. I could see the fear in his eyes.

"Driver's D.O.A.," the trooper said. "Doc, I notice you have a trailer. Could you take the colt and keep him until we can figure out what to do?"

The question caught me completely unprepared. I started to say, *no, he's not even weaned.* But the little colt's frightened look melted away my objections. "Sure."

A moment later the trooper returned with a small white envelope. "These appear to be the foal's registration papers. I found them on the front seat of the pickup." He handed me the envelope. "Look's like he's two weeks old."

One ambulance left with the woman from the Porsche. Soon after, the other took the body of the pickup driver, and a truck from a local rendering plant arrived and removed the mare. Wreckers cleared the highway. Texas State Troopers restarted the flow of traffic.

I loaded the orphan—a scared little colt—into my cattle trailer and started for home.

CHAPTER 2

Driving Home, to Our Ranch in Bushland, Texas

A quarter of a century ago, my wife Maggie and I chose to live in Bushland, population 1,507, a bedroom community located eight miles west of Amarillo on I-40. The leading factor in our decision was 640 acres of grassland listed for sale, three miles north on a narrow blacktop—County Road 2381. We bought the land, called it "our ranch," and built a house and a barn on a bluff overlooking valley pasture that sloped down to Deer Creek, a small tributary that eventually found its way to the South Canadian River. Our ranch had a spacious isolation we both loved.

I turned north off I-40 and called my wife from the car phone.

"You're late," Maggie answered. "I had dinner ready an hour ago."

"I need a little help," I replied. "Could you meet me at the loading chute?"

"Jim Bob, you promised," she scolded. "No more cattle."

"I know," I said. "But this is a horse."

"A horse?"

I smiled, picturing the surprised frown on her face. "And it's only temporary. He'll be gone in a few days."

"What about dinner?" she complained. "It's almost burned."

"Come on, Maggie. It'll only take a minute. Help me unload and then we can have our meal in peace."

I heard a click. Not exactly a positive response, but a resigned statement that she'd meet me at the small pen between the house and the barn. I circled around and backed up to the loading chute as Maggie walked over.

We unlocked the trailer, and as I related the details of the accident Maggie's ire changed to deep concern. When she saw my little cargo, she melted. "Oh, how adorable." That ended any talk about a ruined dinner.

Using our routine developed over the years, we swung the trailer doors back against the wooden fence and fastened them with tie ropes. Good thing. Our frightened little horse bolted. Even a two-week-old colt can be dangerous when he's running wild with hysteria. I knew we needed to do something to calm him or he might injure himself.

Maggie and I both got into the pen with him, and for the next few minutes tried to give reassurance. Luckily, he had a halter, so Maggie grabbed one side and I took the other, doing our best to hold him steady while talking to him in soothing voices. Gradually he stopped bucking and kicking. Maggie rubbed his neck and held him close, her soft touch and gentle voice giving a solace I could never match.

I released my grip on the halter and eased away. Neither the horse nor my wife seemed to notice. They took a few steps together. Then a few more. Little by little they began to walk slowly around the pen. I climbed up on the fence and watched.

"You okay?" I asked as she and the foal walked by a second time.

"We're fine for now."

Maggie had the touch. This two-week-old foal snuggled next to her, walking contentedly as though he'd known her since birth.

Watching my wife mother this colt brought back memories of our daughter Elizabeth as a toddler. It was Maggie who had nurtured Liz, who had recognized her talent, and who—over the years—was responsible for getting her the training she needed to enhance that talent.

"What're we going to feed him?" Maggie asked.

"I'll go fix him a bottle. Be back in ten minutes."

I went inside the barn and prepared formula. Over the years I'd done this many times for calves when a mother cow failed to produce milk. I heated water to a temperature of 110 degrees, as hot as I could tolerate on my hand, and mixed Hi-Pro Milk Replacer, powdered milk, letting the temperature drop between 90 and 100 degrees. Carefully, I poured it into a half-gallon plastic bottle and topped it with a large, three-inch nipple shaped like a cow's teat.

The next thirty minutes was an exercise in frustration.

This colt wanted milk. We tried to give it to him, but he was too scared to take it.

Frustrated, I stepped away. "It's no use."

Maggie stood looking at me in the moonlight. "He'll starve."

"Yes, he might."

"What'll we do?"

"Try again in the morning." Maggie lingered. I pulled her away.

That night I tossed and turned. My apprehensions for the orphan held sleep at bay. The shock of losing his mother, the move to a strange environment, and his refusal to accept the artificial feeding were all signs of overwhelming stress—a condition, if unresolved, would almost certainly defeat his will to live. Someone was going to have to do something.

But it couldn't be us.

We faced another dilemma. Maggie and I were scheduled to leave for New York City in two days. Our daughter was making her debut at the Metropolitan Opera. We weren't going to be around to nurse a baby horse.

CHAPTER 3

Masterson and Associates Veterinary Services, Amarillo

I sat at my desk, sipping a fresh cup of hot coffee, and thought about our problem.

We needed a real horse person. Someone whose love for the equine species surpassed reasonable human expectations, who'd undertake the frustrations of bottle feeding a reluctant foal, and whose personal motivation could be triggered by a starving two-week-old colt. I called Paul Edwards, owner of the world's largest cattle feed yard—Sagebrush Cattle Feeders. He owed me a favor. Most importantly, Paul qualified as a bona fide horseman.

"Paul, my friend, how about a favor?" I asked when he picked up his cell phone.

"The last time I did you a favor, it cost me a pickup," he kidded.

"That's true, but I've never heard a complaint."

"Can't complain about someone who went nose to nose with the bad guys. What's up?"

"Maggie and I need someone to feed our colt while we're in New York."

"Didn't know you had a colt."

I related the orphan story.

Paul might be a billionaire, but he was a real softie when it came to horses. He agreed to meet me at the pen for the orphan's noon feeding.

At twelve o'clock I went home for lunch to find Paul's new Ford pickup parked by the pen. He sat on the fence watching the young colt. "Sure is cute," he said. "How old?"

"Papers say two weeks. Wanna help me mix his formula?"

"Sure."

Paul followed me into the barn and I told him about our lack of success, "Even Maggie couldn't entice him."

"I think the nipple's too big," he said.

"It's what I've always used with calves for bottle-feeding."

"Try using a human-sized bottle and nipple."

"You've tried this before?" I asked.

"Dozens of times. I've been breeding horses for fifty years."

"Ever have a foal that wouldn't eat?"

He shrugged. "Of course. Sometimes there's nothing you can do."

I nodded.

"You have a name for the colt?"

"Nope. He's not ours, you know, but we keep referring to him as the orphan."

"Orphan," Paul repeated. "Not a bad name. Let me carry the bottle. It'll be better if he doesn't see it as we approach."

We walked out into the pen. Orphan moved away—skittish. Gradually we worked him into a corner. I took a firm hold on his halter, hugged his neck and spoke soft words of encouragement. As we began circling around the pen, he seemed noticeably weaker.

15

Paul kept the bottle hidden.

After a few minutes Paul said, "Hold out your right hand."

I did, and Paul squirted some milk into my palm.

"Rub it on his lips, under his nose. Careful he doesn't bite."

Orphan reacted by jerking his head and trying to shake loose from my grip. I held on, tighter.

After a minute or so, Paul said, "Let's try again. Cup your hand so you can take more milk."

I did as he said.

"Now try to splash some into his nostrils so he'll have to lick it with his tongue."

I did that, too.

Orphan coughed and snorted. "He doesn't like my trying to drown him." He jerked his head, pitched, and bucked. "It's all I can do to hold on."

"Do it again," Paul called.

I repeated the whole process.

And again.

Then once more.

Each time the starving horse tasted the warm milk, he bucked a little less.

"You want to try sticking the nipple in his mouth?" I asked.

"Won't do any good," Paul replied. "He's not ready for it. Put away the bottle."

I don't know what I'd expected from Paul, but I was disappointed. The possibility that the little guy might not make it didn't set well with me. As we walked back to Paul's pickup I struggled for something to say.

"Thanks for coming, Paul."

"My pleasure," he replied. "You said you're leaving town?"

"My daughter's singing tomorrow night."

"I read about it in Sunday's paper. Sounds big time."

"It guess it is. Liz has the lead in *Madam Butterfly.*

"Proud Papa takes Mama to the Big Apple to revel in kid's success?"

Paul slapped me on the back and laughed, a big Texas hee-haw. "Don't worry about your horse. I'll take care of the little fellow."

The next morning Maggie and I drove to the Amarillo airport, caught the first flight on American Airlines, and headed to New York to hear our daughter sing. As the plane lifted off the runway, we wondered if we'd ever see Orphan again.

CHAPTER 4

New York City

We hadn't gone any farther than the airport luggage area when
my mother-in-law, Katherine Barrington Smith, started complain-
ing. She objected to our staying at the New York Hilton. I tried to
explain that we needed to be close—the hotel was only ten blocks
from Lincoln Center, while Katherine's apartment, across the river
in Brooklyn, was a distance of several miles. Neither Maggie nor
her mother accepted my reasoning, but when I pointed out that we'd
also lose the deposit on our hotel room, Scottish heritage and a
propensity for conservative fiscal management won the day.
Katherine couldn't stand to see us waste a penny.

Somehow the cost of cab fare didn't matter.

That evening we took a cab from the hotel to Katherine's apartment—the plan was to pick her up, and then the three of us ride
together to the performance. As we pulled away from the hotel,
Maggie used my cellphone to call her mother and arrange the pick
up, but she didn't answer. Assuming Katherine would meet us
downstairs in the lobby or near the front door, we could zip back to

ORPHAN

Lincoln Center.

We were wrong.

Katherine was nowhere in sight.

I left Maggie with the meter clicking off dollars like a Vegas slot machine and took the elevator up to Katherine's apartment on the tenth floor.

"You ready?" I asked, when she answered the door.

"Of course," she answered.

"Maggie's waiting in the cab."

With a haughty gesture, Katherine stepped out into the hall and handed me the keys. "There are three locks," she said.

I fumbled, but finally figured out which key went to which lock.

We rode down in the elevator in silence.

In the cab, Maggie sat in the middle. She and her mother conversed, relegating me to the status of a nonperson being held incommunicado. Fine with me. I was so anxious about our daughter I didn't feel like chitchat.

We found our seats in the third row of the Metropolitan Opera House. Again, Maggie sat in the middle. A good thing, because my nervousness had escalated into profound apprehension. Seeing my little girl on stage in the lead role—hearing her voice fill the theater—caused beads of perspiration across my forehead. My hands turned clammy, and my stomach rolled into a hard knot.

At the end of her first aria, waves of euphoria rippled down my spine. I was so proud of Liz I could hardly remain seated.

"You okay?" Maggie whispered as thunderous applause filled the hall.

I tried to speak. Couldn't. I reached over, put my arm around my wife, and squeezed. Tears rolled down my cheeks.

The clapping gradually quieted.

My mother-in-law handed me a small handkerchief with a look that dared me to soil it. Maggie handed me another. I wiped my eyes and tried to relax. The performance continued and flowed perfectly to the end of the first act.

At intermission, Maggie and I left Katherine seated, and sought a drink of water. Neither of us knew anyone, so no one recognized two strangers from Texas. We mixed with the crowd and listened to people rave about Liz.

They loved her.

My nervousness eased, and we went back to our seats to enjoy the rest of the performance. The house lights dimmed and we settled in, looking forward to one of the most famous and beloved soprano arias in all of operatic literature—"Un bel di" — "One fine day." Instead, we listened to an announcement from the Met's Executive Director, Robert Van House.

"We regret that Elizabeth Masterson is ill and unable to continue. The role of Butterfly will be sung by her understudy for the remainder of tonight's performance." Then he gave the name of the substitute and the page number in the program where her bio was listed.

The announcement hit me like kick in the gut. For a moment I couldn't think.

As murmurs of disappointment rippled through the audience, I turned to speak with Maggie, but she was up and moving away. I hurried to follow, stepping past Katherine. "You coming?" I asked.

She shook her head. "I've paid an outrageous price for this seat. You and Maggie can look after Liz."

Backstage, we found our daughter in her dressing room with a nosebleed. At first I felt relieved to hear her "illness" was something relatively minor.

"Oh, Mom and Dad, I'm so embarrassed," she cried.

I let Maggie lead the conversation. "Liz, Honey, what can we do to help?"

"I don't know," Liz replied. "I just feel weak."

"Weak?"

"Really drained. I can hardly stand. They had to carry me off the stage."

Liz's words tore through me like a fire alarm. I interrupted. "Upset stomach? Nerves?" I asked.

"No," Liz replied. "I'm not a bit nervous. But I'm as weak as a sick puppy. I can hardly lift my arm." She held out her right hand, and we could see what an effort it was. Then her nose started to bleed, again. Maggie handed her a Kleenex.

Someone knocked on the door. I opened it to find a man in a dark suit holding a small doctor's bag.

He introduced himself as the Met's staff physician. "Mr. Van House asked me to look in on Miss Masterson."

I introduced Maggie and myself and invited him into the dressing room. He pulled out a stethoscope, stuck a thermometer in Liz's mouth, and started checking her vital signs. The nosebleed stopped as he questioned her about her symptoms, quizzing her about a bruise on her arm. Finally, he packed his bag and asked me to step out into the hall, closing the door so Liz wouldn't hear our conversation.

"Something's wrong," the doctor said.

I nodded. "Obviously."

"Is she always so pale?" he asked.

Again, I nodded. "No, but...she lives in the city . . . ."

"Extreme fatigue, loss of color, fever, easy bleeding and bruising—all could be symptoms of a deficiency in red corpuscles. I suggest we check her into a hospital and run a complete physical exam."

I felt queasy. Even an old horse doctor like me could recognize the implication of these symptoms.

Leukemia.

CHAPTER 5

MSKCC Hospital, New York City

Memorial Sloan Kettering Cancer Center, one of the most famous medical buildings in the world, stood like a huge neo-renaissance monument near the East River, and our lives changed forever when we took the elevator to the twelfth floor—the leukemia floor. Amid the blue signs and yellow arrows, Maggie and I searched for a miracle for our daughter.

"Acute Myeloid Leukemia," Dr. Strong said, helping us with the pronunciation—MY-eh-loyd—and characterizing the implications. "The prognosis is not good. However, you're at the best possible place for treatment."

Lawrence Strong, MD—a world-renowned oncologist, fiftyish, black, and opera lover—took a special interest in Liz. "These next few days are crucial," he cautioned. "We're giving her a new drug, Imatinib, to try to induce a temporary remission. If she survives, this will give us time to consider a variety of long-range treatments."

For three miserable weeks we watched as they pumped our daughter full of poison. There seemed no end to the vomiting and diarrhea as Liz hung between life and death, all the while her weakened body enduring almost daily puncturing for endless tests.

I called Texas to make arrangements for my responsibilities at home.

Fred Johnson, my associate veterinarian, agreed to cover my practice. He would make most of the routine calls himself. For the big stuff, especially the BSE testing, he'd ask other vets, some of our competitors, to handle the calls.

Paul Edwards insisted on looking after the little horse. He told me not to worry—Orphan was taking milk and would be fine.

Liz's chemotherapy continued. Hoping there would be a future, Maggie and I underwent tests for bone marrow in case a donor should be needed for a transplant.

Liz's case aroused phenomenal attention in our daughter's world of opera. Though she had appeared in only one Met performance, it was enough to create celebrity status and the letters, cards, and packages poured in. Sacks of mail piled up at the hospital. Overwhelmed, I met with New York postal officials and requested that all mail be forwarded to our home in Bushland.

Arranging to be near a loved one in a New York cancer hospital isn't easy. Maggie and I took twelve-hour shifts. During our time off, we'd each return to the hotel for sleep, a shower, and a change of clothes. We regarded each passing day as a victory, a reprieve from the dark cloud that hung over our family.

On day twenty-one—for the first time—the doctor smiled.

"We have two items of good news. She's in remission."

"She's cured?" Maggie interrupted.

"Temporary remission," Dr. Strong cautioned. "The cancer will return."

"She'll have to go through this again?"

Strong nodded, his smile fading to his usual passive face. "It's just a matter of time."

"You said two?" I asked.

"We have a match." His smile returned, and he gestured to some chairs in the corner of the waiting room.

As soon as we were seated, Dr. Strong's smile faded. Holding hands, Maggie and I listened while he gave us a long, solemn Soliloquy on the best-case scenario for Liz's survival—a bone marrow transplant. He didn't say "only," but I could read the implication. His discourse emphasized the dificulty of finding a suitable match. Most BMTs are from siblings and only 75 percent of those are successful. Transplants from other relatives have a lower index of compatibility. For example, the sample they took from Maggie showed a poor match of congruent cells. But mine did not. Miracles do happen, and for some inexplicable reason, my DNA was evaluated as a possible match.

The next few days flew by in a whirlwind of activity, phone calls to oncologists in Amarillo, plans for the future, and most importantly, an upbeat attitude. There was hope.

Sloan Kettering arranged for Liz's transfer to the Harrington Cancer Center in Amarillo. Dr. Seah Lim would be our leukemia specialist there, coordinating treatment with Dr. Strong. During one of our many conference calls, the two doctors explained that the next round of chemotherapy would be needed in about a month, and that the bone marrow transplant should be scheduled in six. Several months of preparation were essential to build Liz's strength.

We discussed plans for Maggie to pack all of Liz's belongings and close her apartment. Liz cried. Our daughter insisted she was *coming back* and she viewed the modest residence on Amsterdam Avenue as a symbol of her return. The cost of maintaining the lease seemed a small price to pay for creating an image of hope, so Maggie made a production of gathering only enough clothes for a temporary move to Texas.

On the morning of Liz's release from the hospital we had a wonderful surprise. Robert Van House, executive director of the Metropolitan Opera, and the entire cast of *Madam Butterfly*, came to see us off. With balloons, streamers, and signs of "Liz shall return," the singers burst into song—the "Humming Chorus," the famous, emotional song from the last act of the opera—as we boarded a stretched black limousine for our trip to LaGuardia Airport.

It was a glorious moment. Liz's spirits soared, but deep down, in the pit of my stomach, I wondered if Liz was seeing Manhattan for the last time.

CHAPTER 6

At Home, "Our Ranch" in Bushland, Texas

If ever in the history of human/equine relationships, social scientists wanted to study an example of "love at first sight," I'd give them an amateur video of Liz meeting Orphan for the first time.

On the morning after we arrived home from New York, Paul Edwards brought the foal from temporary residence at his cattle feeding operation in Sagebrush. He backed his horse trailer up to our gate, and Liz helped us lead the colt into the pen by the barn. Orphan looked great. With a short lead rope attached to his halter, Liz walked him around the small area while Maggie taped the occasion with our little Sony video.

The smile on Liz's face said it all.

Paul watched. I thought he showed a bit of jealousy. "Ten weeks old and the cutest horse in Texas," he said. "I'm gonna miss him."

"Why do you think no one's come to claim him?" I asked.

"Well, I've done some investigating. The AQHA, shows Bobby Garcia as the owner.

"AQHA?" Liz queried.

"American Quarter Horse Association."

Paul turned to me. "Garcia was the pickup driver who was killed in the wreck."

"Yes, but he must have heirs," I replied.

"I looked into that," Paul continued. "Garcia lived in Oklahoma City, had just divorced his wife, and had no children."

For the next few minutes, Paul and I watched as Liz walked the horse in a tight circle. "What about his truck?"

"Joe's Wrecker Service filed a lien against it," Paul replied. "I talked with Joe, and he told me the dilapidated old pickup wasn't worth the cost of having it repaired."

"Still, there must be some salvage value," I said. "Surely, someone will claim it."

"As it now stands, Joe's lien will take it as payment for the wrecker service."

Conversation lapsed again. We watched Liz as she put her arm around Orphan's neck and fed him an apple.

"Surely there's someone out there who wants this horse," I said.

Paul shook his head. "Could be Garcia's heirs aren't horse people, or maybe they think the little fellow's not worth the trouble."

I felt a cloud of suspicion gathering over our conversation. "I wonder if our being in New York and Orphan's temporary move to your feed yard has anything to do with this?"

"Possibly, but I contacted the state troopers and told them where the horse was located."

"No calls?"

"None."

"So, you think he really *is* an orphan?"

"Looks like he's your worry, buddy." Paul looked so happy

about the notion, I thought he might offer me a handshake. Instead, he merely turned his gaze back to the corral.

I couldn't think of anything else to say, so I leaned on the fence and watched Liz as she led the horse, whispering to him. After all the misery she'd been through for the past month, the radiance on her face seemed like a miracle. Orphan exuded a sense of serenity I had not seen before.

These two really liked each other.

Paul noticed it, too. He nudged me with his elbow, "Looks like you've just found the rightful owner."

Things went well for the next four weeks. I went back to work, Maggie outdid herself in the kitchen, and Liz spent her time between going through the sacks of mail and grooming the horse. We laughed, enjoying each other's company.

On day twenty-nine the cancer returned.

This time the disease attacked even more ferociously, and the Harrington doctors prepared us for the possibility that Liz might not make it. We watched helplessly as first the radiation and then the chemo induced another regimen of vomiting and diarrhea. New symptoms of dry-mouth—and sores in her throat—threatened her vocal cords. For four interminable weeks, Liz hung on to life by a slender thread.

Then a month into the chemo, the treatments worked their magic. The cancer lapsed into remission. A week later Liz returned home.

I couldn't tell who was happier—Liz or Orphan.

CHAPTER 7

At Home, the Ranch Near Bushland, Texas

Remission, when it came, provided an idyllic respite from the terror of leukemia. The simple, unspoiled charm of living on a ranch in West Texas with Maggie and Liz—and a foal who we now treated as a member of the family—warmed my psyche and sent me to work each morning with a joy and appreciation for the opportunities ahead. When I could forget the possibility of death, and the likelihood of its imminent return in the next thirty days, I felt an intensity for life unknown in our pre-cancer times. I cherished each moment.

The bone marrow transplant loomed as our only hope. I went to see Dr. Lim to ask if we couldn't do it immediately. As we sat in his office at the Harrington Cancer Center his reluctance surprised me.

"Liz appears strong and healthy," I said.

"Yes," he replied, soberly. He studied me, his classic Asian features hiding all emotional response.

"Two months ago when we transferred Liz from New York, you told us you thought a bone marrow transplant the only solution."

He shook his head, "You're leaving out an important word."

"I am?"

"Probably. I said the BMT would *probably* be the only long-term solution."

I liked Dr. Lim. I didn't like his answer.

For the first time, I thought his medical response semantic, even petty. With anger rising inside, I bit my tongue, both physically and metaphorically, to keep from lashing out. The last thing my daughter needed was a reluctant, irate doctor—one skeptical of her, her family, and her medical needs.

"I just want what's best for Liz," I said.

"Of course. We all do." Again, he studied me, deep in thought.

"Doctor, are you withholding something?"

He remained silent for a few beats. "Yes," he finally said.

This time I didn't bite my tongue. "Damn it. This is my daughter. We have a right to know everything about her medical condition. What is it you're not telling us?"

His face turned white. "I've wanted to tell you. And I've wanted to give your daughter a more candid evaluation of her medical situation. I . . . I just . . . I was waiting for a better time."

"The truth," I said, my voice louder. "*What is it?*"

"The bone marrow match."

"What about it?"

"It . . . it's not as good as we'd hoped."

His answer took all the air from my lungs, and suddenly I couldn't breathe. I opened my mouth to curse, to yell, but nothing came out. He went to a cabinet where a coffee pot rested, poured a small amount, and handed it to me.

"Sip this," he said. "Try to relax."

I tried.

While I sipped hot, black coffee and worked to regain my emotional control, Dr. Seah Lim talked about Liz's medical situation: Yes, a BMT was probably the only long-term answer to her Acute Myeloid Leukemia, as he had not yet found a case where the new wonder drug had led to permanent remission. And, yes, the match between Liz's bone marrow and mine, while it was the best available, remained a poor alternative to a sibling BMT. As recently as yesterday, he and Dr. Strong at Sloan Kettering had reviewed the lab data. The two of them agreed that a transplant using my bone marrow must be viewed as the treatment of last resort.

"What are her chances?" I asked.

"Not promising." He paused. "I'm sorry."

"The last time we talked, you said 25 percent."

"Sloan Kettering, the cancer center with the most BMT cases, told me—at their hospital—only one out of four patients survives a parent-to-child transfer."

"Am I missing something? This sounds exactly like what you told me the first day we walked in the door."

"One thing is different."

"So tell me what it is."

"Test results. Sloan Kettering has developed a new microscopic matching to evaluate the similarity of congruent cells—hers to yours."

"Give it to me in plain English. What are her chances of survival?"

"We can only guess."

"Damn it, give me a number."

"Dr. Strong thinks it less than 10 percent."

CHAPTER 8

Driving Home to Bushland

In a daze, I drove slower than usual—not a conscious decision—just something that happened. Dr. Lim's somber estimate of Liz's chances for survival dominated my mind, my ability to direct willful thinking. I just headed west on I-40, oblivious to to the rest of the traffic.

Truckers didn't like it and honked.

Transcontinental traffic, especially the big eighteen-wheelers running between Chicago and Los Angeles, counted on the flatness of the Texas Panhandle as a stretch to make time. They expected to drive the speed limit plus five MPH—at least seventy-five. So did everyone else—even the Texas State Highway Patrol.

A short "whirr" brought me out of my funk and caused me to look in the rearview mirror where I found flashing red and blue lights. I pulled over.

"May I see your drivers license and insurance papers?" the trooper asked.

I handed him the documents.

As soon as he read my name, he looked up. "Masterson, the vet?"

"Yes, sir." I recognized him. In January, he'd worked the infamous wreck and helped me rescue Orphan.

"How's the baby horse?"

"Doing great."

"Something wrong with your vehicle?"

"No, sir."

"Is there a particular reason you're driving forty-five in a seventy zone?"

"No, sir."

"You aware that you almost caused a wreck back there?"

"No, sir."

He looked at my license. "Is this address correct? Bushland?"

"I'm heading home, the next exit."

He handed back my stuff. "You're legal, but we'd all appreciate it if you'd try to match your driving with the prevailing speed. It's safer."

"Yes, sir. I understand."

"We appreciate what you did to help with the horse." He turned and walked back to his cruiser.

I waited for a clear spot in the traffic, pulled back onto the highway, and headed for home, thoughts moving from cancer to horse. Five minutes later I found a strange car parked in the drive behind my house—a big white Jaguar with New Mexico plates.

As I walked up to the pen I saw Liz, her arm around Orphan's neck, standing near the fence and talking with a big man. Well over six feet, weighing at least two hundred seventy-five pounds, he wore an expensive sheepskin coat, the kind you buy at Santa Fe's renowned Shepler's store. His black beard was well trimmed and he welcomed me with an easy, friendly smile. I guessed his age to be mid-forties.

Liz introduced us.

"Mr. Payne, this is my dad, Jim Bob Masterson. Dad, meet Edgar Payne from Albuquerque. He's a horse breeder."

"Pleased to meet you." He stuck out his hand.

I shook it. His hand completely enveloped mine. "What brings you to Bushland?" I asked, returning his firm grip.

"This little colt." He nodded toward Orphan as he handed me his business card.

I looked at the card.

```
                    Futurity Stables
                 Quarter Horse Racing
                   Edgar Payne, Owner
     Route One              stable 505-555-1234
     Albuquerque 87101      cell 505-555-4321
```

"I understand this colt is the progeny of New Mexico Queen, a mare owned by Bobby Garcia," Payne said.

"Whoa," I said. "I was at the wreck when the mare died, but I don't have any information about her."

He looked down, kicking dirt with the toe of his boot. For the first time I noticed that he wore beautiful, expensive, ostrich boots, shined to a high luster. "I think I can give you that information."

A chill slid down my spine as I realized where our conversation was heading. "Okay, let's hear it."

"On Tuesday, January 17, Bobby picked up his mare and the foal. Bobby told me he was taking them to The Harrah Boarding Stables, a small town on the east side of Oklahoma City. I checked. He never made it."

"You said you have information?"

"This chestnut foal with four white socks and a blaze, was the result of an embryo transplant—an egg from Western Hills Girl, winner of the All American five years ago, sired by First Down Dash, winner of the All American six years ago. I have a copy of the papers and some hair from his tail for DNA."

He handed me a color photo. Even at an early age, less than two weeks old, the distinctive white, diamond-shaped blaze on the forehead made it easy to recognize our horse.

"Expensive bloodlines," Payne gestured to Orphan. "This little colt has the breeding to be a futurity contender. With the right training, he's got a good chance to win the million-dollar purse in a couple of years."

"And what's your interest in all this?" I asked, mentally bracing myself.

"I've come to get my horse," Payne replied.

CHAPTER 9

At Home, Bushland

Edgar Payne eased behind the wheel of his Jag and left.

Liz and I walked slowly back to the house.

We entered a kitchen filled with wonderful aromas—fried chicken and, Liz's favorite, apple cobbler. "What's wrong?" Maggie asked, as she held out her arms and embraced Liz.

Our daughter wept.

I answered for Liz, summarizing the information we'd gotten from Edgar Payne. Then added, "We'll get another horse."

Apparently that was the wrong thing to say. Liz left the arms of her mother and barely made it to the kitchen sink where she vomited. When these attacks occurred, I knew the drill and quickly found a washcloth and towel. Tonight, the retching came in waves of gagging and coughing—what is often called "dry heaves." Her spasms were, I thought, the most severe ever. Maggie and I ended up having to carry our daughter to her bedroom.

Maggie pulled up a chair to sit by the bed. I went to the kitchen and prepared a glass of crushed ice. For the next thirty minutes we stayed with our daughter until she fell asleep. When we quietly went back to the kitchen table where Maggie's beautiful fried chicken dinner had lost its appeal I toyed with my food—trying to force myself to eat.

"At first I thought she was just upset about your comment—that we could get another horse," Maggie said.

"That may have triggered it," I replied. "But this is too severe to be an emotional response to losing the colt."

"You think it's a relapse?"

Maggie didn't say the L word. We both knew a return of leukemia was only a matter of time. She pulled the calendar off the wall and started counting the days. "Her remission started on Saturday, April 15, and she came home on Saturday April 22."

"Yes, I remember."

"Today is May 2." She counted—only eighteen days. The implication came at us like a whisper of death.

I told Maggie of my visit with Dr. Lim. "He thinks as soon as she's stable, we should go ahead with the BMT." I didn't mention his 10 percent.

Maggie squeezed my hand. "Oh, Jim, I just feel so helpless. I wish there was something I could do." A big tear rolled down her cheek, followed by another. Then another.

"There is," I said, aching for my wife, for my daughter, for me.

"What."

"Give her your love and support."

Maggie came over and sat on my lap—putting her arms around me. We sat there, embracing, for several minutes. It was as though we'd reached a plateau, a point where things were either going to get better or worse, far worse, a possibility that terrified me.

"I love you," I said, holding Maggie close, drawing strength from her and she from me.

The next day we took Liz to the cancer center and—for the third time—we braced for the regimen of misery required to kill cancer. Only this time it included me.

For the next three weeks they drained my bone marrow. Much like giving blood, I repeatedly went to the infusion room, a treatment center with a number of reclining chairs where, instead of drawing blood from my veins, they hooked me up to a catheter that drained liquid from my hipbones. For the donor, the feeling is much the same. After each session I felt weak and had to go home to lie down.

In the midst of our battle we received a registered letter. Maggie went to the Bushland Post Office, signed for it, and brought it to the hospital.

Dr. James Robert Masterson
Rural Route 2
Bushland, Texas 79007

Dear Dr. Masterson:
I am writing to thank you for the professional services and personal care you have given to my colt since that unfortunate accident on I-40 last January. I have estimated the following charges:
Veterinarian fees $250
Transportation, accident site to Masterson ranch $50

HARRY HAINES

Daily boarding, 120 days @ $50 $6,000
TOTAL $6,300
Please find enclosed my check in this amount. If you feel that additional fees are due you, please advise and we can negotiate.
I will bring a horse trailer to your pen at ten o'clock a.m., next Tuesday, May 23, to pick up my horse.
Thank you,
Edgar Payne

"What're we going to do?" Maggie asked, alarm coloring her voice.

"I don't think there's any doubt that Orphan is his horse," I said. "So when Payne comes . . . ."

". . . we let him have what is legally and rightfully his."

Maggie clenched her fists. "Liz will be heartbroken."

I thought about Dr. Lim's somber prediction, that Liz's chances were only 10 percent. I started to tell Maggie it probably wouldn't matter. Instead I repeated my suggestion, "We can always find another horse."

Tuesday morning, even though I still felt weak, I went with Maggie to the barn to watch while she fed Orphan. Now weaned, the colt responded eagerly as she prepared a standard ration of grain and alfalfa hay. Maggie joined me on the fence and we watched— what we thought would be—the last feeding.

Our somber reverie was interrupted by an old, white Ford pick-up. A dark-haired woman with chocolate eyes and honey-brown skin, wearing jeans and cowboy boots, got out and walked toward us. In most every way she looked like a working-class woman, one who served food, tended bar, or in some way served the public. The

40

exception to this impression was a white, letter-sized envelope she carried in her right hand. The determined expression on her face told me the envelope represented a mission.

"Masterson?" she asked.

"I'm Jim Bob Masterson," I answered.

She handed me the envelope. "I've come to get Bobby's horse."

CHAPTER 10

At the Pen Behind Our House

I opened the envelope and found a letter addressed to me from a lawyer in Oklahoma City. It stated that Anna Garcia, former wife of Bobby Garcia, had been appointed administrator of the estate of the now deceased Mr. Garcia.

"I'm Anna," she said as she handed me an Oklahoma driver's license.

I looked at it. The photograph was lousy and showed her hair much longer, but I had no doubt she was who she said she was.

"This letter refers to you as the 'former wife' of Bobby Garcia." I returned her drivers license.

"That's what it says," she answered, her voice terse, her eyes flashing.

"Is that different from *widow* of Bobby Garcia?"

"We were divorced." She set her jaw and the emotion in her eyes shot at me like a dagger.

I thought about her answer. I reread the letter and handed it to Maggie. "Looks like we have a dispute."

Anna Garcia's face turned ugly. At first I thought she might come at us, scratching and clawing. She was a large woman, several inches taller than I, and probably fifty pounds heavier. I put my arm around Maggie and puller her closer.

"My lawyer warned me," Ms. Garcia yelled. "He said you would try to cheat me, to take my horse."

Maggie surprised me. Just as I was about to defend myself in a physical confrontation with this large aggressive woman, Maggie stepped between us, using her five feet two inches, 110 pounds, to diffuse the impending altercation.

"Anna, I'm Maggie," she said, in a calm soft voice. "I'll see to it that you're fairly treated."

At first the large woman didn't know how to take this tiny person, only half her bulk. She raised her hand as if to strike—but she didn't.

Maggie stood her ground, and, like a circus trainer daring the tiger, she stared down her adversary.

Anna Garcia lowered her fist.

Then Maggie used her ultimate weapon. She smiled. I've been in fights with my wife and can speak from experience. When she smiles at you, the brightness and intensity of it is completely disarming. You can't win.

Anna Garcia gave up.

The two women looked at each other for a moment, then Anna stepped back. "I have the papers," she said. "The law's on my side."

"Good," Maggie answered. "Let's sit down at the kitchen table over a cup of coffee and call the sheriff."

That's what we did.

After Maggie's call to the sheriff, and while sipping coffee, we told Anna Garcia about Edgar Payne.

Payne's name brought forth a bitter diatribe from Anna. "That lying, cheating horse thief. He's the reason Bobby went to New Mexico to get the mare."

"Tell us what you know," Maggie prompted.

"Bobby worked as a groom for Joshua Smith stables, the biggest quarter horse breeder in Oklahoma. Last year Smith's ten-year-old daughter was in their horse barn when a snake frightened one of the stallions. Bobby pulled the girl to safety—probably saved her life. In rescuing the little girl, one of the horse's hoofs struck Bobby and cracked his shoulder. Mr. Smith wanted to do something nice for Bobby, to show his appreciation."

"So Joshua Smith gave Bobby an embryo transplant?" I asked.

"He had two," Anna said. "The normal procedure is to have multiple eggs fertilized in case the first doesn't take."

"So Bobby had a fertilized embryo implanted in his old mare?"

"Yes, realizing the odds were a hundred to one that old Queenie—that's what he called his horse, New Mexico Queen—would ever get pregnant."

"But she did?"

Anna nodded. "But Bobby made a big mistake."

"What's that?"

"He boarded Queenie at Futurity Stables."

I remembered Payne's calling card. "Edgar Payne's place, near Albuquerque."

Anna nodded. "Bobby told me that as soon as the embryo transplant was successful, he should have driven to Albuquerque and picked up his mare."

"But he didn't?"

"Not right away. He kept hoping he'd get a new pickup. It's over five hundred miles from Oklahoma City to Albuquerque."

"If he never got the new pickup, what changed his mind?"

"Two things. Queenie gave birth, and he heard Edgar Payne was going to pull a fast one. Bobby was afraid he might lose his foal if he didn't get it away from Futurity Stables."

I took a sip of coffee. "How could that happen?"

"Edgar Payne's known in racing circles as a shyster. He's accused of stealing horses, bribing jockeys, fixing races—you name it."

"So, if what you say is true, why did Bobby take his mare there in the first place?"

"Convenience. It's the nearest boarding stable to the vets who do the embryo transplants."

"What about registration?" I asked. Then I told her about finding the papers in Bobby's wrecked pickup.

"Registration has to be certified by the original owner of the embryo. Bobby got Joshua Smith to help him process the papers. The colt has been registered by AQHA. That's what makes him so valuable."

I looked at my watch. Fifteen minutes to ten. Confrontation loomed ahead and I didn't feel well.

Chapter 11

Our Ranch in Bushland

A big white pickup, a Dodge with a diesel engine, pulling an expensive fifth-wheel horse trailer, circled around and backed up to the loading gate of our pen. The trailer had "Futurity Stables, Albuquerque" emblazoned on it in large black letters. Two men got out and swaggered toward the fence to look at Orphan. I recognized one of them as Edgar Payne.

Anna Garcia, Maggie, and I walked from the house toward the pen.

From his actions, I could see that Payne recognized Anna Garcia.

She reacted, too, with open, bitter antagonism.

"Good morning," I said.

"What's she doing here?" Payne asked. I saw a different side to this big man. Instead of the easygoing, friendly manner I remembered from our first meeting, he scowled, the corners of his mouth turning down in an angry snarl. "I hope you know Bobby Garcia divorced her. She's nothing but trouble."

Before I could answer, a Potter County Sheriff's car drove up. Two deputies in brown uniforms got out and walked toward us. Maggie went over to greet them.

"I'm Margaret Masterson," she said. "I'm the one who called you. Thanks for coming."

"You have a dispute over a horse?" asked the first deputy.

Maggie introduced Edgar Payne, Anna Garcia, and me. She then summarized the dispute and showed the deputies the papers and letters we had received.

Payne spoke first. "Officer, even if Bobby Garcia were alive, he would have no claim on this horse." He gave a long, complicated explanation about the transplanted embryo, the fact that Bobby's mare, New Mexico Queen, was only carrying the foal, and that these papers proved his ownership of the colt.

Payne's transformation amazed me. Seconds ago he came across as a bully consumed with rage, a powerful horse owner ready to pulverize anyone who got in his way. Now, speaking with these deputies, he seemed a gracious, well-meaning person, victimized by others, seeking help with people who were stealing his horse. It was a skillful performance. If I were a deputy, I'd have given him the horse outright.

Anna Garcia could see what was happening and quickly stepped in to present her side, but she made a mistake. She became defensive. Her face reddened, and as she had with me earlier that morning, she lashed out at the two deputies. "You're in cahoots with this guy," she yelled. "I can see you're going to cheat me and take my horse."

I wouldn't have been surprised if she had physically attacked both deputies. Evidently they thought it a possibility. Both stepped back.

"I have a suggestion," I said.

Anna paused.

The two deputies looked at me.

Edgar Payne frowned.

"Why don't we turn this over to the courts? Let a judge hear both sides and determine who owns the horse."

"No, that's unnecessary," Payne responded. He spoke calmly and in a convincing voice. "Those papers clearly show my legal status. This horse belongs to Futurity Stables."

"No. It's Bobby's horse," Anna shouted. "You have the papers that show I'm entitled to the remainder of his estate." She moved toward the deputies.

"Officers, at considerable expense, I have brought my horse trailer over 300 miles to be here this morning," Payne said. "We should take the horse to Futurity Stables where he will have the best in professional care. If there's a dispute, this woman can make her case in New Mexico courts, and if she wins, she can come get the horse."

"No," Anna screamed. "No!"

Maggie came over and put her arm around my waist. "How're you doing?" she whispered. "You look pale."

"I think I'd better find a place to sit," I said.

"Officer, my husband's a donor for a bone marrow transplant," Maggie said. "We need to go inside."

Together, she walked me to the kitchen door. On the way we could hear Anna's high-pitched voice shouting obscenities.

Inside, seated at the kitchen table, we watched out the window as the minutes passed.

Edgar Payne's big diesel pickup and trailer left. Then Anna

Garcia's old, white Ford pulled out. We heard a knock at the door. Maggie opened it to find one of the deputies.

"What happened?" Maggie asked.

"A Mexican standoff," the deputy replied.

"So?"

"So we decided to take Dr. Masterson's suggestion and let Judge Gleeson settle it."

"What about the horse?"

"Would you be willing to keep him until we get a legal ruling?"

Maggie turned and looked at me.

"Sure," I said.

"They're both mad at you," the deputy said. "I think they're going to sue."

I shrugged and thought about Liz. With my daughter so ill with cancer, the last thing I needed was Orphan being taken from her.

CHAPTER 12

In the Hallway Outside Liz's Room,
Harrington Cancer Center, Amarillo

"We should know something soon," Dr. Lim said.

"Soon?" I asked.

"In the next few days." He shook my hand by holding it with both of his, as if to say, *don't give up hope.* Then he embraced Maggie, patting her on the back, another gesture that communicated his empathy. Then he left.

Maggie and I went into the room and stood by Liz's bed. She looked emaciated, colorless, frail. Maggie reached over to stroke her face. Liz didn't react. Had our daughter given up—so weak she no longer cared about her appearance?

"Your grandmother's coming to see you this afternoon," I said. "She'll expect every hair to be perfectly in place." My weak attempt at humor about Liz's shiny bald head.

Liz tried to smile. It pained me that this vibrant young woman was now so weak she couldn't. I put my hand on hers and gave it a little squeeze. "Dr. Lim says remission is just around the corner."

Liz turned and looked the other way. She knew it was a lie.

Maggie glanced at her watch. "It's time to go to the airport."

I nodded.

"Your mother will ask why you didn't come to pick her up."

"And you'll tell her I stayed to be with Liz."

"She won't like it."

"Tough shit."

"Jim Bob."

"Yes, dear?"

"You don't have to be so crude, and in front of our daughter."

I looked at Liz. The corners of her mouth now turned up, a stronger semblance of a smile than I had seen in days. Not her normal, big toothy grin, but a reaction that told me she still had a will to live. I patted her arm, "Be back in a minute."

Maggie and I walked to the car. Yesterday, when Katherine called us, Maggie suggested she visit Liz. Maggie didn't actually say the words, "Liz is dying," but the implication was certainly there. And I had to give Katherine credit—she loved Liz and would do anything for her. She immediately said she would come. Ten minutes later she called back to give us her flight schedule.

Now, standing at the car, Maggie held out her arms. We embraced and held each other for a few minutes as if, together, we could somehow protect our daughter. It was a memorable moment, a time when communication defies verbal expression.

We closed with a kiss. Maggie left to drive to the airport and I went back to hospital room where I found Liz asleep.

An hour later, the door opened, and Maggie brought her mother into the room.

"Oh my God," Katherine gasped. Like all of us, she had not

expected Liz's stark, gaunt appearance.

I put a finger to my lips. "She's asleep," I cautioned.

Katherine went to the bed and gently placed her hand on Liz's shoulder. It was a poignant moment, one filled with emotion, concern, and doubt.

Finally, Maggie spoke, "There's a coffee room down the hall."

Katherine turned and nodded.

Maggie looked at me with pleading eyes. "You coming?"

Reluctantly, I did so.

With the three of us seated around a table, Katherine started in. "New York has the best hospitals, the best doctors," she said.

I looked at Maggie.

"Why on earth would you bring your daughter, *my only grand-daughter*, to this God forsaken part of the world?"

I started to say something. Maggie put a hand on my arm and shook her head.

"Second-rate hospitals, third-rate doctors. It's practically a death sentence," Katherine continued.

"Mother, there're some things you don't know," Maggie said.

"I can see. With my own two eyes I can look at her condition. Anyone can tell Liz is not receiving proper treatment."

I stood to leave.

"And her father runs away."

Counting to ten, for Maggie's sake, I ignored Katherine and made my way back to Liz's room where I found Dr. Lim, smiling from ear to ear.

"What is it?" I asked, afraid to hope. "Why the smile?"

"This morning's blood test," he said. "She's in remission."

Dizzy, I grabbed the nearest chair and fell into it.

"This means we can start the BMT as soon as she's strong enough," he continued.

"A permanent cure?" My voice trembled as I voiced the question.

"A *chance* for a permanent cure. If all goes well, we'll know something in about a year."

Emotion came over me like a tsunami. My whole body tingled with such intense elation I couldn't move. Dr. Lim put his hand on my shoulder. "Your wife in the coffee room?"

I couldn't speak. I nodded.

"You want me to give her the this information or do you want to tell her yourself?"

"You . . . you go . . ." Then I thought about Katherine. The scenario of relating these facts tempered my emotions. I could speak. "Wait, I've changed my mind. I'd like to be the one to share the results."

"Tomorrow you'll see a big difference." His smile widened. "Liz will probably be ready to go home in a week." He gave me that double-handed handshake, and as he went out the door I thought I could see a bounce in his step.

I walked down the hall with my thoughts churning over what words to use—how to relate this to my mother-in-law. Dr. Strong at Sloan Kettering had said Liz's chances were only 10 percent. Yet our so-called second-rate hospital and third-rate doctors had pulled her through . . . *and* a permanent cure danced on the horizon.

And I got to be the one to tell Katherine.

CHAPTER 13

At Home in Bushland

Katherine stayed a week. But even her whining and carping couldn't put a damper on our good news. We rejoiced as a family that our daughter had made it into another thirty-day remission. Especially, we celebrated the scheduling of her bone marrow transplant. At last, we had the possibility of a permanent solution. There was hope.

Three weeks later, the entire BMT procedure took place on a single day and seemed like an anticlimax. Similar to a blood transfusion, Liz reclined in a lounge chair in the cancer center's infusion room while the oncology staff hooked her up to a catheter. Maggie and I watched through a window in the door as the plastic pouch— one filled with my bone marrow—dripped life-saving white liquid into her system.

A week later, Liz came home, and—although the three of us could look back on a number of high points in our life together— none could surpass the euphoria of that evening. I grilled steaks. Liz opened a bottle of champagne. Maggie baked a cherry cobbler that

ORPHAN

would have made George Washington's mouth water.

But our euphoria was short-lived.

The next morning a Potter County Sheriff's car pulled into the lane by our house, and a deputy came to the door with two official-looking envelopes. Maggie and I sat at the kitchen table and learned that I was the target of two lawsuits.

Edgar Payne, of Albuquerque, was suing me for theft of a horse, for slander, for personal expenses attributable to the recovery of his horse, and for damages to his business reputation.

Anna Garcia, of Oklahoma City, was suing for theft of the same horse—a circumstance that, to my limited legal knowledge, seemed unreasonable. Her complaint also listed obstruction of justice, cruelty to an animal, and emotional pain and suffering which she said she endured during my possession of the horse.

I went to see Paul Edwards to ask him for the name of a good lawyer.

"I've been hearing some gossip about you and the horse," Paul said.

"Good or bad?"

"Let's just call it juicy."

He poured coffee. I waited for him to continue.

"Word has it your cute little colt has expensive bloodlines."

"Whoa. I don't even know if I have a horse."

"That's another bit of gossip."

"Really?"

"People out at the American Quarter Horse Association tell me you're the most favored legal target in the horse world."

I grimaced. "That's why I've come."

"How many law suits?"

"Two," I answered. "You know any good horse lawyers?"

He chuckled. "That's a specialty I'm not too familiar with." He smiled as he ripped open a small pink package of artificial sweetener and dumped it into his coffee. He looked down at his cup and stirred. "The juiciest part of the local gossip is that you'll be joining the racing circuit."

I laughed. That was the furthest thing from my mind.

"Trainers, jockeys, grooms—the whole bit," he continued, obviously making fun of me.

I shook my head, a gesture to squelch his mockery. "Seriously, Paul, I'm looking for advice. I don't know many lawyers—none that have expertise in resolving disputes over horse registration and ownership."

Paul quit laughing. "Neither do I," he said, "but my buddies at AQHA do." He picked up the phone on his desk and dialed a number from memory.

I listened to Paul's half of the conversation for about five minutes and watched as he made notes on a scratch pad. When he finished, he slid his scribbles across the desk to me. I found the name Suzanne McDonald and a phone number.

"She's expensive but considered the best."

"A woman lawyer?"

"She's a true horse person. Whenever the association has something really contentious, that's the name they call."

Smith, Shrader, Thompson, Zachary, and McDonald, L.L.P., had offices on the fifth floor of the Bank of America Building in downtown Amarillo. In fact, they took the entire floor—the top level in what was regarded as one of the most beautiful buildings in Texas. The diamond-shaped structure occupied an entire city block and was built around a huge center atrium with full-grown trees reaching toward a glass-skylight ceiling.

The receptionist pointed across the treetops. "She's in 517—the far corner."

As I began the hundred-yard hike, looking out over the atrium's greenery, listening to the sounds of artificial waterfalls, I had the urge to hold on to my wallet. This was a place that reeked of expensive fees. It seemed incongruous that my good intentions to help a baby horse could have led to this.

We had no plans to claim ownership of Orphan. I had no interest in racing. We couldn't afford trainers, jockeys, and all the rest of the encumbrances required for a competitive quarter horse. As I entered the office of Suzanne McDonald, Attorney at Law, it seemed obvious that the time had come.

I had to find a way to sever Orphan's relationship with the Masterson family.

CHAPTER 14

The Offices of
Smith, Shrader, Thompson, Zachary, and McDonald, L.L.P.

Suzanne McDonald was a knockout.

"I'm Suzie," she said as she held out her hand.

I don't know what I was expecting, but when this beautiful woman introduced herself, I reacted with temporary dementia. I shook her hand, but I couldn't think of anything to say. All I could do was stare.

"You must be Dr. Masterson?"

Towering above my five foot-seven—I estimated her height at six-one or two—with a perfect figure, dark eyes, gleaming white teeth and silky black skin, she reminded me of a contestant in the Miss America contest. She wore a white, knit turtleneck with tailored black slacks. Her clothing emphasized all the curves, especially her breasts. I listened with my mouth open as she tried again to start conversation.

"You're *not* James Robert Masterson?"

I looked up to make eye contact. "Jim Bob," I answered. "In the

Texas Panhandle, everybody calls me Jim Bob."

She laughed, and I was surprised at the husky, low-timbre of her voice. "All my clients call me Suzie." She led the way into her office and closed the door. "What can I do for you today?"

I handed her the papers.

She pulled out a pair of reading glasses with heavy, black horn-rimmed frames. The eyewear transformed her appearance—now she looked intellectual, like the archetypal star of a television show that featured Hollywood lawyers. She read for a few moments, then looked up and asked, "Would you like coffee?"

"Sure," I replied.

She picked up her phone and punched a button. "Mary Lou, would you get us two cups, and the works, please?" She returned to scanning the two lawsuits.

A secretary brought us each a cup of coffee in ceramic mugs with the law firm's initials, S-S-T-Z-M, in bold, white letters. I wondered how much extra it cost to provide drinks in monogrammed coffee cups.

Suzie read.

I sat and sipped.

When she finished, she dropped the papers on her desk and smiled at me. "Looks interesting."

"Before we get started, could we discuss fees?" I asked.

"Two-fifty an hour."

"Eh . . . I'm not sure I can afford you. How many hours?"

"Whatever it takes. No way to know at this point, but the scuttlebutt is that you have an expensive horse, so you probably shouldn't be talking to a cheap lawyer."

"Scuttlebutt?"

"The horse community is a small world. I've heard about you and your horse through the AQHA."

"Orphan isn't *my* horse."

"From what I can see, from a preliminary look at these two case summaries, I don't think the horse has an owner."

"In that case, what happens?"

"When a person dies intestate and there are no heirs, property reverts to the state."

"In-tess-tate?"

"Without a will."

I tried to think about the the various outcomes for Orphan. "Would you give me some possible scenarios? Especially, what happens if the horse becomes the property of the state?"

She took a long drink from her coffee cup, as though she needed support to deal with a slow learner. "First you have two lawsuits. If Payne proves his case, the horse goes to him. Or if Garcia proves *both* that the horse should go to the estate of her ex-husband and that she has legal jurisdiction to administer all property—which is really a stretch—then she will take control."

"But you don't think Orphan's going to either?"

"If you had only one lawsuit, it might have had a squeaky possibility. Sometimes a judge will rule to settle a suspicious suit—even a spurious effort like one of these—just to clear the books. When it's contested, as this one certainly is, I don't see that either has a snowball's chance."

"So if Orphan is declared property of the state, then what happens?"

"He'll be sold at auction to the highest bidder. And you can file a claim for your expenses to be paid from the proceeds." She pulled out a yellow pad and started making notes. Then she pushed the pad toward me. I read her projected figures.

Daily boarding fees, 345 days @ $50 = $17,050
Veterinarian fees 500
Transportation fee, site of accident to stables 50
Attorney fees 2,400
TOTAL $20,800

"You really think Orphan will bring that much at auction?"
"At least. It could easily be twice that figure."
"Wow."
"How much do you know about quarter horse racing?"
"Not a thing. Actually, I've never attended a race." I hedged. "But I've watched a couple on TV.
She shook her head and looked away.

CHAPTER 15

Driving West on I-40 Toward Home

I thought about Orphan and wondered if I could afford to bid on him—a big, multiple if—should the opportunity present itself.

The answer seemed obvious. At a probable cost of $20,000, the response would have to be "no." If Suzanne McDonald's prediction of $40,000 should develop—and while I thought it remote, it was not impossible—the reply was a resounding "hell, no."

An easy *financial* decision.

However, another consideration—racing—kept resurfacing. For the hundredth time my brain went through the pros and cons. First, I didn't know anything about horse racing. Second, I really didn't want to learn. Third, I couldn't afford such a venture. End of story? Well, I had one other consideration—Liz.

If this decision affected my daughter's emotional well being, I'd do whatever it took, but I hoped it wouldn't come to that. Anyway, where could I get $40,000?

I parked by the kitchen, walked back to the barn, and found Liz grooming Orphan.

"How's he doing?" I asked, delighted to see some color in Liz's cheeks.

"Fine. The farrier just left."

"Horseshoes?"

"Not yet, but soon." As she talked, she ran a brush through Orphan's mane, combing it until it glistened. "How'd it go with the lawyer?"

"It went fine," I lied.

She stopped brushing and looked at me, waiting.

Orphan turned and nuzzled her.

"Dad, come on. Give." She resumed brushing. Orphan raised his head in appreciation. "Will one of these characters be able to take this guy from us?"

"Probably not. Our lawyer thinks that neither claim has merit, but if he isn't awarded to one of them, the state gets him to auction off."

Liz brightened, stopped brushing, and looked at me "So we could bid on Orphan?"

"That's a possibility."

I braced myself for the next question.

She didn't ask it.

Both of us were silent for a few minutes. Orphan sidestepped closer to Liz. It was almost as if he had understood the conversation.

"We'll just have to cross that bridge when we come to it."

Liz resumed brushing. "I understand."

I walked back to the house.

"Why the long face?" Maggie asked.

I went through all the details.

"We can't spend $40,000 on a horse," she said.

I nodded. "The lawyer, says the trial won't come up for a while."

+++++++++++++

Three months later, Suzie McDonald called. The next day I drove to a meeting in her plush office in downtown Amarillo.

"We have a date for the hearing," she said as she passed a stack of papers across her desk. "Next Tuesday, nine o'clock, room 401 of the old Potter County Court Building."

I read the heading on the top sheet.

Ex Parte Injunction: A restraining order to halt the Sheriff's Sale of a horse formerly owned by Bobby Garcia.

"What's this?" I asked. I flipped through the document filled with legal mumbo-jumbo.

"Basically, those papers hold four legal actions."

"Four?"

She nodded. "First, Edgar Payne has filed to stop the State of Texas from selling the horse. That's the *Ex Parte* Injunction."

"What's *Ex Parte*?"

"The other side's not present. Bobby Garcia is deceased."

I turned to page two. "Next?"

"The second is Payne's civil lawsuit for conversion. He contends that James Robert Masterson illegally took possession of his property—a horse—and has been holding it wrongfully. He's seeking money damages and the return of his horse."

I shook my head in disgust. "That's ridiculous. I was only trying to provide shelter for a foal whose mother was killed."

"So you say."

I looked at her in disbelief. "It's the truth. Everyone who knows anything about the situation will confirm it."

"Jim Bob, you'll have to prove it."

"No problem," I said, thinking of the officer at the scene of the accident.

"But, there's more."

"Good God, what else?"

"Look at the third page. Elizabeth Garcia says her former husband Bobby still owed her money from the divorce. She's seeking to intervene in the 'Payne vs. Masterson' lawsuit with a prior claim."

I scanned the document filled with legal phrases I couldn't understand. My eye caught a figure of $50,000 in the third paragraph and the term *mental anguish*. "You'll have to explain this."

"A variation on the same theme," Suzie replied. "Garcia says that her ex-husband withheld details of valuable property in their divorce proceedings, and, had she known of the impending birth of this valuable horse, she would have been entitled to file for ownership."

"Fine with me. Let her have it."

"There's more. She says you conspired to hide the horse, that this action has caused her great mental anguish, and that you should pay her damages in the amount of $50,000—and return the horse immediately."

I threw the papers down on her desk in anger. "This is ridiculous. All I've done is try to help."

"Let's go to the last page," she replied, her manner and voice ignoring my frustration.

Reluctantly, I picked up the packet, feeling revulsion at the touch, and tried to decipher the legalistic jargon on the final page.

A Petition for Interpleader Status.

"I assume you want three things," Suzie said. "You want the horse to go to its rightful owner, you want to be reimbursed for the expenses you've incurred, and you want these charges against you dismissed."

"Will this Interpleader thing do that?"

"It's one way. Essentially, you are asking the court to take possession of Orphan."

"What's the other way?"

"Ways. There are two. You could file a countersuit asking for damages from these two people who are hassling you. Or you could seek ownership of the horse—a lawsuit where you compete against Payne and Garcia."

In a nanosecond I made the decision.

"I want the court to take the horse."

CHAPTER 16

Potter County Courthouse, Amarillo

Liz didn't come to the hearing. Maggie stayed home to be with her. I went alone to face Edgar Payne and Anna Garcia.

Well, not exactly alone. I met my expensive lawyer in the hallway outside the courtroom. We sat on one of the wooden benches to discuss last-minute strategy.

"You haven't changed your mind?" she asked.

"No," I replied.

"You don't want the horse?"

"I can't afford him."

"So, our goals are to aid the court in determining who owns the horse, to fight off any claims against you, and to seek reimbursement for your expenses?"

"Suzie, I'm just trying to be a Good Samaritan. That's been my intent from the beginning. At this point I don't feel like one."

"I know, but we still have to prove that you don't and never did have any ulterior motives."

My three witnesses walked up—Paul Edwards and two Texas

State Troopers. Suzie and I stood. The five of us shook hands.

"Any questions?" she asked.

No one spoke as she looked around the circle, making eye contact with each of us.

"Here we go, then." The four of us followed her into the courtroom.

The Potter County District Courtroom was old and famous. In the 1970s it had been the site of the longest and most expensive murder trial in Texas history when a Fort Worth oil billionaire named Davis won acquittal for the murder of his wife. Davis, reportedly the wealthiest person ever to be tried for murder, hired Racehorse Haynes as his attorney and paid millions for a spectacular defense. Even today, more than a third of a century later, critics referred to the verdict as, *not guilty by reason of wealth.*

My first impression of the large room was its smell. A musty odor harkened to past battles where lives hung in the balance, fortunes were distributed, and hordes of people came to watch. A wooden railing divided the room into distinct areas—one part for the participants, the other for the audience. The spectator section was at least twice as large, and I estimated it would seat over a hundred people on antique wooden benches.

An elevated desk dominated the front of the courtroom. A large, high-backed chair flanked by two flags—a U.S. flag on one side, a Texas flag on the other—left no doubt where the judge would be seated. Directly in front of the judge's bench, centered in the room, was a raised platform and chair with a placard that read "witness stand." I assumed the small table and chair nearby were for the court reporter. A uniformed bailiff, wearing a gun and a badge, sat at a small table by the window. A wooden railing separated the jury box with its twelve chairs along the far wall. Since this was a "non-jury" civil suit, those chairs would remain empty.

In the center of all this were three large tables, each with two chairs. Payne and his lawyer sat at the first. Garcia and her lawyer took the second. Suzie and I headed toward the third. As we passed the others, we paused to shake hands. Formal introductions and stiff body language left no doubt about the presence of an adversarial relationship. I looked at my watch to see that it was almost nine o'clock.

The bailiff stood and in a loud, commanding voice, directed, "All rise." A door on the east wall opened and a large, heavyset man in a black robe entered. The bailiff announced, "The forty-seventh district court of Texas is now in session, the Honorable David Gleeson presiding. You may be seated."

Judge Gleeson used his microphone. "I now call for final hearing of Potter County Case number 63,104, Payne vs. Masterson. Are the parties and their witnesses present and ready?"

The lawyer for Payne rose. "Plaintiff ready."

Garcia's lawyer stood. "Intervening plaintiff ready."

Suzie joined the others. "Defendant ready."

The judge nodded to the bailiff.

"Would all witnesses please stand," the bailiff commanded.

I looked around. Practically everyone seated in the audience, about a dozen people, stood.

The judge interrupted. "Principals who will testify must also stand and take the oath."

I stood along with Payne and Garcia.

"Raise your right hand," the bailiff said. "Do you solemnly swear the testimony you give in this hearing will be the truth, the whole truth, and nothing but the truth? If so, answer, I do."

In unison, we responded, "I do."

"Be seated."

Everyone sat except Suzie. "Your Honor, the defendant wishes to file with the court our petition for Interpleader Status. You have our paperwork."

Immediately, Payne's lawyer stood. "Sidebar, your honor?"

The judge motioned with his hand, inviting the lawyers to come forward. They gathered around the end of the judge's desk and conferred. I could hear whispers, but understood nothing. A few minutes later the sidebar ended, and the attorneys returned to their seats.

"I'll take the defendant's petition under advisement and give you my decision at a later time. Meanwhile, I suggest all parties proceed with the assumption that this item will receive the court's favorable ruling." He turned to Payne's lawyer. "Call your first witness."

I looked at the big clock on the wall and saw that it was nine-fifteen. For almost six hours—except for fifteen-minute breaks in the morning and afternoon, and an hour break for lunch—we listened to Payne's lawyer and Garcia's lawyer hammer away at me, at what they called my dissolute and immoral attempts to steal their horse. When I first came into the courtroom, I thought my side of the story unimpeachable. Now I wasn't so sure.

Suzie called her first witness—me.

She asked how I happened to take Orphan to my ranch. Why I had kept him for almost a year. What I was seeking in this trial.

Then she called the two state troopers. Each in turn confirmed my story, that they had asked me to take the horse, that Potter County had no facilities for the care and feeding of a two-week old foal, and that they had visited my ranch and found I had taken good care of Orphan.

Paul Edwards testified about the trauma of a young horse losing its mother, the difficulty of bottle-feeding, and his opinion that I should be commended for raising the young colt to its present healthy status.

When we came to the end of the day, I felt better. Suzie and I stayed to talk about the case.

"What do you think?" I asked.

"Looks like Anna Garcia's got a lock on the horse."

"Oh?"

"Did you see the look on Payne's lawyer's face?"

"No, I guess I didn't."

"It was the look of defeat. He couldn't compete against a poor woman who'd been short-changed in an unfair divorce settlement."

"Good for her."

"Bad for you."

"Why do you say that?"

"She probably doesn't have resources to reimburse you for the care you've given Orphan."

I thought about it for a second. "That's okay," I said, meaning it.

"Jim Bob."

"If she can come up with enough to pay legal fees, I'll be happy."

"You're due almost $20,000 for taking care of Orphan."

"Can we negotiate?"

"Of course."

"When the time comes, let's try to make it easy on her."

"She wasn't going to take it easy on you. She was suing for $50,000."

"Yeah, but I'll bet that was her lawyer's idea," I said with a smile.

Suzie's facial expression turned defensive—fierce, belligerent. I guess my attempt at lawyer humor wasn't funny to the tall, intellectual, attorney.

Chapter 17

At Home in Bushland

Through a haze of sleep, I thought I heard a phone ringing.

It rang again, louder. Maggie punched me. "It's for you."

"How do you know?" I mumbled.

Another ring.

"At two o'clock in the morning, it's always for you."

I fumbled for the light. The answering machine started. "We're unable to come to the phone right now, but you can leave a message. Wait for—"

"Hello," I said, my voice low, raspy.

"Dr. Masterson, this is Wyatt Reed, Amarillo PD, homicide."

I sat up on the side of the bed. "Say again?"

"Jim Bob, this is Wyatt. We worked together on the murder of Congressman Young."

I looked at the red numbers on the clock by our bed—2:16 a.m. "Sure, Wyatt, I remember, but why are you calling me?"

"Do you know a woman named Anna Garcia? Drivers license says she lives in Oklahoma City."

"Well, I sorta know her. We're involved in a lawsuit."

"Could you ID her?"

An alarm bell went off in my head. I hesitated. "Probably. Why do you ask?"

"She's dead. We found your name among the papers in her room."

I took a deep breath, feeling my heartbeat accelerate. "Dead? Where?"

"Room 212 at the Motel 6. We'd appreciate your help in identifying the body."

"Now?" I gasped. "It's two in the morning."

"Yes, sir, and you might want to bring your attorney."

"Wyatt—"

"How about some advice from a friend?" he interrupted.

Suddenly speechless, I didn't reply. It seemed obvious he was going to give it to me whether I wanted it or not.

"It would be best to have your attorney present for questioning."

I found my voice. "Questioning? About what?"

"Murder. Anna Garcia was strangled with a wire."

"Good God."

"These papers indicate you held an adversarial relationship with Garcia."

"She was suing me for possession of a horse. Surely that doesn't make me a suspect in her murder?"

"Jim Bob, try to see it from my perspective. You're one of the few people—maybe the only person—in Amarillo who knew her. I have to question you."

Maggie turned on the light on her side of the bed. "A suspect in *what* murder?" she asked.

"I'll be there in thirty minutes," I said hanging up.

Grabbing some clothes, I told Maggie what I knew, and called Suzie. She agreed to meet me at the Motel 6. When I arrived at the motel's parking lot, I counted four vehicles with flashing red and blue lights—one ambulance and three Amarillo police cruisers. I found Suzanne McDonald in the lobby. Even without makeup—and wearing jeans, sneakers, and a University of Texas jacket—she looked as glamorous as ever.

"Tell me what you know," she said, leading me over to a corner away from the occupied front desk.

I did, and groused about being questioned as a suspect.

"He's just doing his job," Suzie replied. "Let me do the talking."

"At two hundred and fifty dollars an hour, I'm not sure I can afford your talk."

She chuckled. "At three o'clock in the morning, I have a special rate."

"Oh, no."

"For you it's free. So relax and let me answer his questions."

"Free?"

She took off toward an outside stairway. I followed. A uniformed policeman escorted us to the second floor and led us to room 212 where we found a beehive of activity. Wyatt gave us each a pair of booties—plastic covers for our shoes—and led us into the room to identify the corpse. The body lay on the floor in the middle of the room, draped with a white sheet. He lifted the cover.

I recoiled at the sight of the purplish, swollen face, but there was no doubt. Both Suzie and I identified Anna Garcia.

Wyatt Reed led us to an adjoining room where we sat down around a folding table. He pulled out a small tape recorder, turned it on, and laid it in the middle of the table.

I looked at Suzie.

She put her hand on the switch, and I heard a soft click. "Before we start, let's lay some ground rules."

Wyatt frowned. "Jesus, Suzanne, we have to interview him."

"My client will agree to answer facts. No questions about opinions, about what he thinks happened, or who might have done it."

"Damn it, what's he got to hide?"

"Nothing. But all questions about opinions must be submitted in writing—to me. Dr. Masterson is currently involved in legal proceedings with others who knew her, some of whom you might consider suspects. He has to be careful that he maintains a position of strict neutrality."

She turned on the tape recorder.

Wyatt's face reflected his irritation, but he began his questions. He asked my name, address, occupation, and a number of innocuous facts. Before each response, I looked at Suzie and if she nodded her head, I did my best to give a brief answer. If she shook her head, I declined.

"Can you account for your whereabouts last night from seven o'clock to midnight?" Wyatt asked.

"Yes," I replied. "I was at my home, three miles north of Bushland."

"Who can attest to that?"

"My wife Margaret and my daughter Elizabeth."

"Anyone else?"

"No."

"Any phone calls?"

I paused. The night had been one of those rare occasions without interruptions. "No."

I thought about the thousands of times when cattlemen had called, an intrusion on my family—part of my professional life.

"Who do you think might have murdered Anna Garcia?"

I looked at Suzie. She shook her head.

I wanted to say Edgar Payne. But I didn't.

CHAPTER 18

Two Weeks Later, Masterson and Associates Veterinary Services

Ida Mae Campbell, my secretary, came to the door of my office. "Suzanne McDonald, on line one," she said.

"Good morning, Suzie," I answered. "How much is this costing me?"

"We bill by the quarter hour," she said. "The minimum for this consultation, if you keep it short, will be $62.50, but you'll think it's worth it. I have some good news."

I pondered the kind of news that would be worth $250 an hour.

After a few seconds, she asked, "You still there?"

"Okay, let's hear it."

"Judge Gleeson put everything on hold."

"What does that mean?"

"He says that since one of the litigants has been murdered, and the other is a suspect, he's not going to rule on either suit until the murder has been resolved and a guilty party brought to justice."

My thoughts immediately flew to the colt. "What about Orphan?"

"He directed the sheriff to find food and shelter for the horse—at county expense—until we resume legal proceedings."

"What does that mean? Where will they take him?"

"I called the sheriff. He wants you to look after the horse. Will you do it?"

I didn't have to think twice. "Of course."

"And I'll run a tab for your legal expenses."

"Really?"

"Have you kept up with how much you've paid me so far?" I heard a smile in her voice.

Suddenly I realized the total was zip. I'd been so worried about *how much,* I'd failed to realize that I had yet to write a check. Before I could offer to make a first payment, she changed the subject.

"You heard anything more from the APD?"

"No. What about you?"

"I talked with Wyatt," she said. "He has no leads."

"Surely he's investigating Edgar Payne."

She hesitated, the kind of hesitation that warned me I wasn't going to like her answer. I waited.

"First," she said, "there is no evidence linking Payne with the murder. Second, he has an alibi."

I wondered about his alibi, but at the same time a thought ran through my brain. It wasn't worth $250 an hour to hear about it. I changed the subject.

"So what about me? I have an alibi, too," I said.

"Mmm hum," she offered dismissively. "You'll continue to be *a person of interest* until the crime is solved."

"In other words, I'm still a suspect?"

"Don't worry about it," she said.

"Of course I'm worried about it," I countered.

"Look. Their list is like flypaper. Once you're on it, it sticks."

"Yuck."

"I said don't worry about it."

"At two-fifty an hour, easy for you to say."

She didn't answer. Instead, I heard a sharp, hiss, an intake of breath. After a minute of uncomfortable silence, I asked, "You still there, Suzie?"

She exploded. "Jim Bob, you are the most ungrateful, lousy, cheap sonovabitch in West Texas. You're facing a possible murder charge over a million-dollar horse, and you're worried about $250? I'm busting my butt trying to give you adequate legal representation, and all I get are penny-pinching, petty, skinflint complaints."

"Suzie, I'm sorry—"

"Maybe it's time for you to find a new lawyer."

I could see that our banter was edging way too close to the line, and I wished we were having this conversation face-to-face. "Have you heard the story about the new client who went to see his famous lawyer—one with very high fees?"

She was silent for a moment, and I sensed she was trying to analyze my question for veracity. "No," she finally replied.

I went on with the story.

"'Can you tell me how much you charge?' asked the client.

"'Of course,' the lawyer replied. 'I charge $250 to answer three questions.'

"'That's a bit steep, isn't it?'

"'Yes, it is,' said the lawyer, 'and what's your third question?'"

She laughed. Not a big Texas guffaw, but enough that I could tell my attempt at levity had softened her resentment.

"I really do appreciate all you're doing for me."

"Gee, is that a word of thanks I hear?"

"Don't let it go to your head."

"But all this gratitude . . . what's a girl to do?"

"Tell me more about million-dollar horses."

She chuckled. "If a two-year-old wins the All American Futurity, the big race held on Labor Day in Ruidoso, New Mexico, that's the purse. A million dollars."

Mentally, I did some fourth-grade arithmetic—10 percent of a million would be $100,000. Then I asked, "Would you take 10 percent of Orphan's winnings in lieu of your usual hourly fee?"

Her answer came back instantly. "Sure."

"You're serious?"

"Want me to draw up a contract?"

"Suzie."

"What?"

"Have you forgotten about the Interpleader stuff? I don't own the horse. I don't want to own him. Hell, you wrote the petition to the court asking the state to take him."

"I haven't forgotten," she said.

Then she chuckled. I pictured her with an impish smile, like she knew something I didn't.

CHAPTER 19

At the Pen by Our Barn

The months rolled by uneventfully.

Amarillo PD's murder investigation stalled out.

Judge Gleeson refused to do anything about the lawsuits.

Orphan grew from foal into yearling, a beautiful young colt. That spring he reached 90 percent of his adult size and weight.

Liz took over complete care and responsibility of the horse. She gave him TLC on a daily basis, and he became the main concern of her existence. I thought it a blessing and an aid to her recovery.

Liz's health seemed robust. Her hair grew back, and she radiated energy. She read books on equine care and grooming, on the medical needs, feeding, and especially the training—of racehorses. As each month passed, cancer problems retreated farther into history and the "C" word ceased to exist in our family conversations.

Life on our little ranch resumed a happy, almost boring routine. On the first Monday in May, I watched Liz heft a saddle onto Orphan, and—like a normal father—I worried.

"Why don't we get a professional trainer to do this?" I asked.

"Dad. He trusts me, and I want to do it."

I'd learned not to argue with my daughter on two topics—on the techniques of singing and on the care and nurturing of horses. I sat on the fence and fidgeted as she led Orphan around the pen, getting him used to the feel of saddle and bridle.

Later that afternoon, still worried about my daughter's safety, I drove to Sagebrush to visit Paul Edwards.

"Jim Bob, it would be better to get a trainer, someone who's experienced in breaking a horse. It could be dangerous."

"I understand that. That's why I'm here."

"So?"

"So Liz wants to do it all by herself."

"People don't always get what they want."

"Try telling that to a cancer survivor."

Paul's face turned into a question mark. "What's that got to do with riding a horse?"

"When life becomes uncertain, priorities shift. Liz loves Orphan. She wants to do this more than anything else in the world."

"Oh." Paul looked down for a moment. "You're not exactly asking for my advice, then? You're looking for a way to say yes?"

I nodded.

He came over, put one boot on the bottom rail of the fence, and pointed to a swaybacked mare, the worst looking horse I'd ever seen. "That old Chestnut's Nellybelle," he said, "and I'll loan her to you until you get Orphan broke."

Later that afternoon I left Paul's ranch with an earful of advice and his fifteen-year-old Nellybelle. Gentle as an old dishrag, we eased her into the pen with Orphan, and I followed Paul's advice that a second horse, one being ridden, would make it easier to break

Orphan—to get him accustomed to carrying a rider.

Paul was right.

The next morning, when Liz sat in the saddle on Orphan for the first time, nothing happened. All my apprehensions turned out to be for naught. So with Liz on Orphan and me on old Nellybelle, we circled the pen for five minutes and then dismounted. Liz pulled the saddle and the bridle from Orphan and gave him his favorite treat—an apple. We did this every day for a week, each time a few minutes longer until, on the seventh day, we opened the gate and rode out into the pasture.

After a gentle, thirty-minute ride to the far end of the field and back, we returned to the pen where I found Paul Edwards sitting on the fence.

I dismounted Nellybelle to visit. "Thanks for loaning us your training horse."

He smiled. "That old nag has to do something to justify her feedbag."

"With her around, Orphan never bucked, not even once."

"You had something else going for you."

"The rider?"

Paul nodded. "She's light. She's familiar, and you've got a smart horse."

"You think if someone else tried to ride him, Orphan would buck?"

"Like a wild stallion."

"So, when the time comes for Edgar Payne or someone else to take him, you think the new owner's in for trouble?"

"In the horse business, we call it training."

"Someone will have to train Orphan to accept other riders?"

"And a dozen other things."

"Such as?"

"Racing. Competing with other horses. Experiencing the starting gate. Traveling in a horse trailer. Living in the stables at a race track."

Paul's assumptions about Orphan's future bothered me. "We haven't decided that he's going into racing," I objected.

Paul smiled and gave a small shake of his head, a gesture of incredulity. "Jim Bob, this is an expensive horse. Whether it's you or the next owner, no one can afford to keep him as a pet. He has to race."

Liz came for Nellybelle. Paul and I silently observed as she led the old mare into the barn to unsaddle and brush her down.

As we watched, Paul commented. "Your daughter looks good."

I nodded. "The doctors say we're just about over the BMT."

"BMT?"

"Bone marrow transplant. The medical standard is a year. After that, it's considered permanent."

"How long's it been?"

"Eleven months."

"She looks so healthy, one would never guess she's a cancer survivor."

"We're not using the word survivor much—yet."

Maggie walked toward us holding the cellphone. "Your lawyer," she said.

Paul offered his goodbyes. Maggie handed me the phone.

"What's happening?" I asked.

"Judge Gleeson called. "He wants to see us. Can you meet me at the courthouse tomorrow morning, ten o'clock?"

"Sure. Any idea what's up?"

"Yes."

I waited, and heard a long, low rush of air conveying bad news.

"Edgar Payne has written a letter asking the judge to rule on his lawsuit."

86

CHAPTER 20

Potter County Courthouse

Judge David Gleeson welcomed Suzie and me into his inner sanctum—the *judge's chambers*. It was the first time I'd seen him without his black robe. He looked surprisingly non-intimidating— less like a stern authority figure, more like a kindly, gray-haired, compassionate advisor. After handshakes, Gleeson sat behind his big desk. My lawyer and I took chairs facing him. The smell of rich leather gave the meeting an ominous sense of future importance.

"Payne is pushing hard for a ruling," Judge Gleeson declared.

"Is there some kind of legal statute about how long a judge can legally delay proceedings?" I asked.

"No, but—" He turned to Suzie, as though he expected her to answer my question.

I, too, looked at her.

As if on cue, Suzie picked up the explanation. "If Payne thinks he's being stiffed, treated unfairly by Judge Gleeson, he can appeal."

Gleeson gave a benevolent smile acknowledging my ignorance without his having to put it into words. "Judges don't like to be overturned by a higher court."

"We're ready to resume the hearing," Suzie offered.

"All right, how about three weeks from today?" he asked.

Suzie looked at me. "Okay?"

I nodded. "Whatever."

Judge Gleeson wrote it into his calendar. "I'll notify the attorneys for both Payne and Garcia."

His comment surprised me. "You know that Anna Garcia is now deceased?" I ventured.

"Yes, but officially she's still a part of the hearing," the judge replied. "And she may have relatives that will continue to press her position as intervener."

I rolled my eyes. I couldn't believe it. It seemed unfair that someone could continue her lawsuit against me from the grave.

"Anything else?" he asked.

"No," Suzie replied, but looked at me for the final say.

I shook my head.

"See you in three weeks. Tuesday morning at nine o'clock."

Suzie and I walked to the parking lot.

"Anything you want me to do?" I asked.

"We've made our case," she replied. "All we can do now is appear before the judge."

She got into her car, a little red Mazda Miata, and drove away. I piled into my big white Chevrolet Suburban and headed for work.

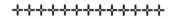

For the next three weeks, I hardly thought about the lawsuit, until, on Monday evening, the day before the scheduled hearing, while I sat at the dinner table with my wife and daughter, Suzanne McDonald called.

"Tomorrow morning, meet you in the courthouse hallway, five minutes until nine?" she asked.

"Come again?"

She sighed, and I visualized her rolling her eyes. "Potter County Courthouse. The hearing."

"Wow. Thanks for calling. I almost forgot."

Suzie lectured me.

I apologized.

"What was that?" Liz asked, as I hung up the phone.

"Edgar Payne is attempting to reopen the lawsuit against me.

"He still wants Orphan?" she asked.

I nodded. "Same as before."

"What are his chances?"

For a moment I didn't respond as I thought about how to frame my answer. Liz's reaction told me I'd made a mistake. Her expression fell, her shoulders sagged, and she slumped back in her chair. She had mistaken my hesitation as acquiescence. To her, I was giving away her horse.

Too late, I said, "We're just setting a date for the next round of discussion. It'll be months before we know what's to become of Orphan."

Liz wasn't listening. She rose from the dinner table and hurried to the bathroom. Almost immediately we heard the familiar sounds of retching and repeated flushing of the toilet.

"I'd better go check," Maggie said, alarm in her voice and in her expression.

Trying to stay calm, I beckoned, "Call me if I can help."

In a matter of a few minutes, Maggie summoned me and, together, we helped Liz to her bed. Maggie pulled a chair to her side and held her hand. I went back to the bathroom to clean up the mess. Thirty minutes later, exhausted, Liz fell asleep. Disheartened, Maggie and I returned to the kitchen. She cleared the table and loaded the dishwasher. Then I called the doctor.

Months ago, after the bone marrow transplant, Dr. Seah Lim, our leukemia specialist, had given me a card with both his office and home phone numbers, and asked that I call if Liz experienced any signs of a relapse.

"What are her symptoms?" Dr. Lim asked.

"Vomiting, diarrhea, and abdominal cramps," I answered. "The diarrhea is much worse than before."

"Redness of skin?" he asked.

"I've not noticed any skin rashes or redness." I looked at Maggie for confirmation.

"Wait," she interjected. "Let me speak to him."

I handed her the phone.

Maggie practically strangled the receiver, she gripped it so tightly. "Liz's abdomen has a rash, a very definite redness of skin," she said.

I could only hear one side of the conversation, but before the conversation ended, Maggie acknowledged that we would have Liz at the Harrington Cancer Center the next morning.

I called Suzie McDonald and told her I couldn't be in court the following morning. My daughter's leukemia had returned with a vengeance.

CHAPTER 21

Harrington Cancer Center, Amarillo

The next morning Maggie and I took Liz to the cancer center. Immediately, a team of six professionals, headed by Dr. Lim, whisked her away leaving us with the admissions clerk. After completing the paperwork, I joined Maggie in a familiar place—the hospital's waiting room.

Waiting is the bane of cancer treatment. Even my experience as a bone marrow donor paled by comparison to the agony of being confined to a small room, hoping for the best, expecting the worst, yet feeling powerless to do anything to help a loved one. The unknown loomed with foreboding consequences as we waited to hear about Liz's relapse.

Maggie, bless her, tried to comfort me—one inconsolable to another.

"What's taking so long?" I asked, my nerves wearing thin.

Maggie checked her watch. "We've only been here a little over three hours."

Three hours. It seemed like we'd been waiting an eternity. "Did Dr. Lim say how long it would take for the tests?"

"You know he didn't."

"Damn, it shouldn't take this long."

"Shall we go for more coffee?"

I shook my head and tried to remember how many cups we'd had. Five? Six?

Just as it seemed we'd never hear, Dr. Lim appeared. Maggie and I stood. I tried to read his face. I couldn't. As usual, his features remained inscrutable. He pulled up a chair and gestured for us to sit back down.

I hoped he'd say something about Liz's condition. Instead he asked a question. "How much do you know about Graft-versus-Host-Disease?"

Maggie looked at me. I shook my head. I knew a little, but wanted a complete explanation from an expert. "Nothing," she replied for both of us.

"GvHD," the doctor continued, "is a condition that sometimes occurs following a bone marrow transplant. It happens when the donor's transplanted marrow makes antibodies against the recipient's tissues. These cells try to destroy the host as if it were a disease."

"How serious is this?" Maggie asked.

"GvHD can be acute or chronic, mild or severe. Severe cases can be life-threatening."

When he said the last two words, a cold chill rippled down my spine. I wanted to leave—to walk away from more bad news.

Instead I asked, "Have you been able to evaluate Liz's case?"

The doctor sighed, a clear indication of his frustration with our questions. "Too early to say. We'll know more in a few days."

"Can you give us some general idea?"

"When GvHD develops, white cells from the BMT, in this case the marrow you gave to Liz, attack the host's tissues—in this instance, your daughter. The usual targets are the skin, bowel, or liver. In Liz's case, we've found major loss of cells that cover the inside of the bowel, leading to loss of fluids and proteins from the body. The cramps start when a large area of bowel has lost its cover—the mucous membrane—and it becomes difficult for the patient to fight off bacteria and fungi."

"Do you have a plan for treatment?" I asked.

"Corticosteroids," he replied immediately. "Cortisone-like steroids that provide relief for inflamed areas of the body. They lessen swelling, redness, and allergic reactions."

"Side effects?" I asked.

"Of course. Corticosteroids are very strong medicines, and the side effects can be serious. I'll have the nurse print out a list for you."

"How soon will you be able to tell us if this is life-threatening?"

He shook his head. "Leukemia is always threatening."

Maggie entered the conversation. "But surely you can give us some idea?" Her plea came with an edge, an urgency to know something. "Even a guess would be better than nothing."

"We do have the Seattle system, a grading that was developed at the Fred Hutchinson Cancer Center in Seattle in the 1970s. Points are given as a percentage of total skin that's inflamed. Intestine involvement is determined by the amount of diarrhea per twenty-four hours. And liver is graded by the serum level of bilirubin. The mildest level of GvHS is grade one—the worst is grade four. Survival of patients with grade three is problematic. Grade four is almost always fatal."

The doctor's words—always fatal—came at me like a dagger to the heart. I put my arm around Maggie and held her close as I asked, "What is Liz's level?"

Dr. Lim looked at the floor and frowned. "As I said, it takes time to evaluate. We may have enough data for a preliminary diagnosis in a couple of days."

Maggie and I looked at the doctor. He seemed to want to say more. We waited.

He cleared his throat. "I do have one *potential* bit of good news."

"Please, doctor," Maggie begged. "We need any good news you can give us."

"A reversed rejection is possible. While attacking the tissues of the patient, the new stem cells may also attack the cancer cells. This phenomenon is called 'graft-versus-leukemia effect.' If that happens, it means a permanent cure—no relapse into acute myeloid leukemia."

Maggie and I reacted with stunned silence. My mind replayed his words as I tried to reassure myself that I'd heard what he said.

"*If* this happens, the cancer will be gone," he repeated.

"Permanently."

Chapter 22

The hospital Cafeteria

The doctor said we wouldn't be able to see Liz until late afternoon or evening. He suggested we go for lunch, so Maggie and I trudged down to the hospital cafeteria. I don't know why we bothered—neither of us felt like eating. I glanced at my watch to see that it was almost one o'clock.

It was a surprise when Suzanne McDonald walked through the cafeteria door.

"How's Liz?" she asked as she pulled up a chair.

"We don't really know," I replied. "The next few days will tell."

"Is this a relapse of the leukemia?"

I nodded. "The official name is Graft-versus-Host-Disease."

She asked for an explanation, and I summarized what Dr. Lim had told us.

"So if it's bad, it could be really bad—but if it's good, she could be cured?" Suzie asked.

"Yes, that's the gist of it," I replied.

"And you'll know in a couple of days?"

"More," I answered. "The doctor says we'll know *more*."

She glanced at the two of us with deep sympathy in her face. "Anything I can do?"

"Nothing to do but wait."

We sat through a few uncomfortable moments of silence. I had the impression she wrestled with ideas about conversation.

I cleared my throat. "I have a feeling you didn't come here just to inquire about Liz. Is there something else on your mind?"

She shifted in her seat. "Do you feel like discussing the Payne lawsuit?"

"Sure." I glanced at Maggie. "It'll give us something to take our minds off cancer."

"I have some good news for you—that's why I wanted to come here and deliver it in person." She smiled a little half-smile. "I thought it might give you two a lift."

"We'd welcome a bit of good news," I replied.

"This morning Payne helped us," Suzie said.

"Really?"

"Unintentionally," she explained. "When the judge asked about your absence and I told them of Liz's leukemia relapse, Payne acted like a horse's ass."

"How?"

"He criticized you. Said a daughter with leukemia was no excuse. His comment was so insensitive that it really ticked Judge Gleeson."

"What happened?"

"The judge changed his mind."

"Go on."

"When we started the meeting, I thought Gleeson was ready.

Garcia's lawyer had sent a letter dropping out of consideration. And if big-mouth had kept quiet, I think the judge would have given his ruling."

"But he didn't?"

"No, he asked me when your daughter would be out of danger."

"And?"

"I told him thirty days."

"Where'd you get that?"

"I remembered what you told me about the attack in New York City—that it took thirty days for Liz's medication to work into remission."

"What did the judge think?"

"He postponed the hearing for thirty days."

"Did Payne react?"

"He was livid."

For the first time in 24 hours I laughed. It felt good.

"Like I said," Suzie continued, "Payne really ripped it with Judge Gleeson."

"What do you predict?" Maggie joined the conversation.

"I think the judge will rule that neither Garcia nor Payne have proven ownership. That means the horse will revert to state ownership."

"And be sold at auction?"

Suzie nodded. "At a Sheriff's Sale, probably in ninety days."

"Wow."

"You two want to make a bid?"

"No, but our daughter might."

"Ninety days, plus some time to set up the sale—at the most, four months." Suzie smiled. "Tell her to hurry and get well."

After Suzie left, Maggie and I returned to reality . . . the waiting room.

That evening they let us visit Liz. She looked awful.

As we stood by our daughter's bedside, Maggie holding Liz's hand, I thought about how little my concern over the ownership of a horse mattered. Life was too fragile—our future too uncertain.

Liz raised her hand toward me, a feeble gesture, but an unmistakable request. She wanted me to hold her hand, too.

I took it, and I felt her pulling me toward her. As I lowered my head she whispered, "Are we going to lose Orphan?"

Chapter 23

Harrington Cancer Center, Amarillo

Nothing changed. One, grim, depressing day followed another as our daughter lay in her hospital bed. Heavy medications complicated Liz's symptoms and made it difficult for the doctors to make accurate readings of her tests.

At first, she passed more than a gallon of watery excrement in a twenty-four hour period—a terrible indication of the GvHD rejection in her intestines. In subsequent days, as the amount lessened, Dr. Lim cautioned, "This may only be the result of the corticosteroids."

"When will we know?" I asked.

"When test results show steady, day-by-day improvement."

"Her diarrhea is consistently less," I commented, clinging to hope.

"Yes, and that's good. However, the rash is spreading and total skin inflammation has grown worse."

I took a moment to let that settle in. Then I asked, "What about the liver?"

"Her bilirubin serum level has been erratic," the doctor answered. "She's been here four days. After the first test, the level went down, the second up. Today it was down."

"What can we do?" I looked away, not wanting him to see the emotion in my eyes.

"Give it some time." Then in a gesture of support, he placed his hand on my shoulder for a moment before turning and leaving the room.

That night I tossed and turned. Sleep refused to come. I got up. Showered and shaved, dressed, and went out to check on Orphan. After feeding him, and as the sun peeked over the eastern horizon, I loaded him in our cattle trailer.

At breakfast, I made a suggestion. "Why don't we take Orphan to the hospital parking lot and walk him?"

Maggie looked at me, her face tense with fear. "Why?"

"So Liz can see him," I gave Maggie the brightest smile I could muster.

Maggie smiled back. "She'd like that."

That's what we did.

For the next week, each morning we loaded the horse into the trailer and drove to the cancer center. Then we'd take turns. One of us would go up to the second floor to Liz's room, pull back the curtains, and roll her bed over to the window so she'd have a full view of the parking lot, while the other paraded Orphan back and forth among the cars.

The first day Liz reacted well. She smiled. It was a weak facial expression, but a positive one.

The next day, her smile was a little stronger.

By the end of the week, even the doctor noticed.

And the test results improved.

When we came to the end of the second week, Liz asked if we could run the horse. I tried. With a lead rope on Orphan's halter, I ran from one end of the parking lot to the other, flat out. For Orphan this was an easy pace. For me it was exhausting.

Orphan's reward was a piece of apple after each lap.

My reward came that evening when Dr. Lim asked for a conference with the three of us.

"I have some good news," he said. "And some *potentially* better news."

I felt my pulse quicken. I grabbed Maggie's hand and held on.

"As you know, the diarrhea's gone."

Maggie nodded.

"The rash is clearing. I think it's a definite indication that we've turned a corner."

Maggie squeezed my fingers so hard it hurt. I didn't care.

"And best of all, the bilirubin tests now show a consistent, day-after-day trend toward normal. I think she can go home tomorrow."

Maggie released my hand. I held out my arms, and we embraced.

"Hey, do I get to be a part of this celebration?" Liz asked, elated by the news.

We hugged our daughter and then I looked back at the smiling Dr. Lim. "You said 'potentially better news.' What did you mean?" I asked.

Dr. Lim hesitated. "Let's be careful how we interpret this," he cautioned.

"Okay, careful," Maggie repeated.

"The emphasis has to be on *potential*," the doctor continued.

"We understand."

"That's because we won't know for sure for at least a year."

"A year?" Maggie and I raised the question in unison.

"I've seen too many cases where patients and their families jump to conclusions and then, and in the year that follows, have their hopes dashed with devastating results."

"Okay, enough with the suspense," I prodded. "What's is it?"

"These symptoms are consistent with 'graft-versus-leukemia effect.' If it continues for a year, it means Liz is lucky. She has a permanent cure."

CHAPTER 24

At Home on Our Ranch, Bushland, Texas

October weather in the Texas Panhandle can be among the most satisfying on earth. Overnight lows in the fifties, afternoon highs in the eighties, little or no wind, and beautiful sunny skies to lift one's spirits. That fall was the best I could remember.

Not that Liz needed any incentive, but the gorgeous weather seemed to help her improve. Day after day she grew stronger and reveled in her return to a normal life. God had given our daughter a new outlook.

A central aspect of her increasingly better health was Orphan. Liz took him out for a ride in the field every morning. Even a horse can tell when things are going good. He carried a joyful look in his eye as Liz fed and groomed him. I watched and thought things couldn't be better.

Until the morning Suzanne McDonald called.

"Judge Gleeson wants to meet with us," she said.

"Uh oh," I replied.

"Time for a ruling, Jim Bob."

"When?"

"Next Monday morning, nine o'clock."

"Bad news?"

"Maybe not, but the judge needs to bring these lawsuits to closure. In case you haven't checked your calendar, it's been a year since Payne and Garcia filed."

"What about the murder investigation?"

"That's another reason to end this. Nothing's happening. Probably never will."

"So what do we do next?"

"So, I'll meet you next Monday."

That weekend I attempted a number of times to bring up our court case in conversation with Liz and Maggie, usually at a meal. However, each time I tried to broach the subject, their exuberance over our current state of affairs warned me off. I didn't have the guts to become the bearer of bad news. On Monday morning I went alone to the Potter County Courthouse to meet my lawyer.

Much had happened during the past year, but our courtroom remained the same. Same musty smell. Same three tables arranged exactly as I remembered them. Same places for Suzie and me at the last table, just as we had for the original hearing. Payne and his lawyer also took their same places.

One change—the chairs at the Garcia table were empty.

No one else was present in the courtroom except the bailiff and the court reporter.

"All rise," the bailiff commanded.

Judge Gleeson entered wearing his black robe—a determined expression on his face—and took his chair.

Everyone sat.

"Bailiff, please pass out the material," the judge ordered.

Copies of a two-page legal document were distributed to each person.

"The attorneys for Anna Garcia and her estate have withdrawn their intervening suit," the judge continued. "Therefore, this case reverts to the plaintiff, Edgar Payne, and his charge that the defendant, James Robert Masterson, illegally took possession of his property—a horse—and has been holding it wrongfully."

Suzie reached over, and with her pen, marked a paragraph near the bottom of the first page.

I read the text as the judge pushed on, his words crisp, authoritative, "I find, however, that the plaintiff has failed to meet a judicial burden of proof in his claim for ownership of the horse."

The sound of ruffling paper filled the room as everyone turned to the second page.

"Therefore, in light of this ruling, I do hereby order the following actions." Gleeson paused.

Again, Suzie used her pen to mark my document. This time she circled four, short, numbered paragraphs at the end.

Gleeson read them aloud.

"Number one, that the withdrawal of Anna Garcia is accepted."

I looked briefly at the empty table.

"Number two, that the defendant's Petition for Interpleader Status is accepted."

The court reporter typed away, her face expressionless. Again, no reaction from anyone.

"Number three, that the Petition for Conversion, for ownership of the horse et al, from Edgar Payne is denied."

Movement at the next table caused me to look up. I saw Payne's face twisted in anger. His lawyer stared down, rereading the document, shaking his head.

"And number four, that the horse, by default, becomes the property of the State of Texas and shall be sold at the Potter County Sheriff's Sale to be held on the first Tuesday in January. Proceeds from this sale shall be used, as much as possible, to defer the expenses of maintaining the horse—for providing shelter, food, and care."

Payne's lawyer stood. "Your honor, we object."

"Objection noted," the judge replied.

"We plan to appeal."

"Better do it quickly. Announcements for the sale will go out immediately and the sale date is only a little more than two months away." He rapped his gavel. "Court adjourned."

The judge left, followed by the bailiff and the court reporter.

Payne huddled with his lawyer.

Suzie led the way, and I followed her out into the hallway.

"What'd you think?" I asked.

"I think you got everything you asked for," she replied.

"What about his threat to appeal?"

"Probably nothing but a bluff."

Just as she said the word "bluff," the courtroom doors burst open, and Payne stomped out, followed by his lawyer. I've seen anger many times in my life, but rarely like this, and never in the formal setting that surrounds a courtroom. He came straight at me, eyes blazing, his fist held ready to strike.

"You're nothing but a piss-ant troublemaker," he roared. "You wouldn't know what to do with this horse if you got him."

Speechless, I did the only thing I could think of. I stepped in front of Suzie.

Payne glared at me for a moment, then tromped heavily down the hall to the elevator. He pressed the button, turned, and yelled back, "If you think you can outbid me at the auction, you're sadly mistaken."

The elevator doors opened, and he left.

Suzie shrugged. "I guess Payne expects you to bid against him for the horse."

"What else is new?" I asked.

"Jim Bob, you need to be careful. This guy seems irrational to me."

"Irrational?"

"Crazy," she said. And when she said the word she looked straight into my eyes.

CHAPTER 25

At Home on Our Ranch, Bushland, Texas

Our balmy October weather turned into a November blue norther. The temperature fell sixty-five degrees in one afternoon from a noontime high of seventy-five to an overnight low of ten degrees. The next morning we found all the leaves from our mulberry tree on the ground.

At the breakfast table I tried to impress my daughter with a famous quote, "Will Rogers, who once visited the Texas Panhandle in the 1930s, was reputed to have said, 'There's nothing between Amarillo and the North Pole but a barbed wire fence.' Then, as the story goes, a crusty old rancher replied, "And it's down.'"

Liz looked at me with a blank expression. "Who's Will Rogers?"

I shook my head and thought about whether or not it was worth answering.

Liz smiled at me, put on her heaviest coat, hat, and gloves, and went out to the barn to care for Orphan. Maggie poured us a second cup of coffee and asked, "What're we going to do about this auction?"

I hesitated, sipping the hot coffee.

"That horse means everything to Liz," Maggie added.

I nodded.

"How much do you think it'll take to buy him?" she asked.

"At first, I thought $10,000 or less," I replied.

"At first?"

"Suzie thinks $20,000 is a more likely figure. Could be higher."

Maggie's face fell.

"She heard a guy at the AQHA say it could go as high as $40,000."

Maggie gasped. "Who in their right mind would pay $40,000 for a horse?"

"The name Edgar Payne comes to mind."

I could see my wife becoming distressed—she clammed up. Her forehead wrinkled, her eyes narrowed, and her face clouded into a scowl, warning me to keep out of her way.

Silently we loaded breakfast dishes into the dishwasher.

I decided to test the waters. "Last night I worked on our financial statement."

Maggie finished loading the machine, added detergent, closed the door, and flipped the switch.

"Our net worth is showing a little over $100,000," I continued.

Maggie leaned back against the kitchen cabinet and crossed her arms over her stomach. "How can that be?"

"I took the appraisals of our home and the veterinary clinic, subtracted the amounts of the mortgages, and listed the difference as our equity. Then I made an estimate of the value of our cars and personal belongings. Finally, I added the market price for our herd of Black Angus. All of this totaled $100,000. Theoretically, that's what we're worth."

"That's just on paper," Maggie said. "I looked at our checking account. The balance was $982 as of last night."

"If we decide to buy Orphan, we'll have to go to the bank and borrow the money."

"How will we pay it back?"

"Out of his winnings."

"Winnings?"

"Racehorses are an investment. People borrow money to buy them expecting, if they win races, the horse will make money."

"That's like borrowing money to gamble."

"Yup."

At that point I lost Maggie completely. She gave me the full force of her silence and stomped off to brush her teeth, leaving me to ponder the ramifications of entering the Masterson family into full-fledged gambling.

I poured another cup of coffee and looked out at our daughter and her horse. Wisps of white vapor came from each as their breath mingled in the cold, still air. Moments later Maggie strode back into the kitchen and put her arm around me. Apparently, she'd thought things over and calmed down a little. We watched as rider and horse galloped out into the field, completely oblivious to the cold.

"I'd like to go to the bank and set up a line of credit so we can bid on Orphan," I said.

"I knew that's what you were leading up to," Maggie replied.

"We have to do this. It's for our daughter."

She chuckled. "Don't think I haven't noticed."

"Noticed what?"

"You love that horse as much as she does."

CHAPTER 26

Texas State Bank, Amarillo

"You want to set up a line of credit?" asked Patrick Conway, the bank's chief loan officer.

I handed him the financial statement Maggie and I had carefully prepared, showing our net worth of $102,423. "That's right," I said.

He scanned the sheet with a practiced eye. "How much?"

"As much as the bank will allow."

Conway lowered the financial statement and locked eyes with me. "Banks like it better when you have a specific amount in mind. I assume you want this money to expand your business?"

I hesitated, and then replied, "Well, sorta."

He looked back at the statement. "Jim Bob, that's not a good answer."

"I want to expand my veterinary business into equines."

He nodded. "Okay, tell me more. How do you plan to do this?"

"I want to buy a horse."

"A horse. Singular? Just one animal?" He laid the financial

statement on his desk, removed his glasses, and stuffed them in his coat pocket.

"Yes, I want to bid on one that's going to be sold at the Potter County Sheriff's Sale in January."

His body language changed. From a gregarious, open, welcoming attitude, highlighted by an upbeat facial expression that anticipated business—he shifted to a cautious, hesitant, guarded banker, a persona dedicated to protecting the bank's resources from risky investments. He swiveled his chair away from me, back toward the coffee pot on his credenza, and grabbed a cup.

"Coffee?" he asked.

"Sure," I replied. "Black."

He poured two cups and handed one to me.

"I think I know the horse," Conway said. "One of our bank's board members is a vice-president of the American Quarter Horse Association. He and I have talked about the horse you've been boarding—his history, the wreck, the lawsuit, and the upcoming sale in January."

I nodded. "That's the horse. What does the AQHA say about it?"

"They want to do a story about him in next month's *AQHA Journal*."

"And?"

"He thinks the sheriff is too little and too late. The time to sell this horse was last September in Ruidoso, at the big, three-day, national auction, where they have 500 or more racehorses on the block."

"What does he think will happen at this sale?" I asked.

"Probably only a handful of bidders will attend. Mostly local. Good news for you, as the horse will bring only a fraction of what it would have sold for in Ruidoso."

"Did he give you a figure?"

"Nope."

"Even a guess?"

"I think I can quote him. He said a horse is worth what two people agree on—the seller and the buyer." Conway took a long draw from his cup.

"Back to my line of credit," I said. "What do you think?"

"Jim Bob, we have to look at this from the bank's viewpoint."

"I agree. You see me as your customer. One who wants to borrow money."

"Yes, and you've been a good one. We want to keep your business."

"But—"

"But this ain't business. You're asking for money to buy a racehorse."

"It's an investment."

"No, it's a gamble, and people are supposed to use their discretionary money for gambling."

"Pat, I don't have enough cash to bid on this horse."

"Then maybe you shouldn't bid." He turned back to the credenza, lifted the coffee pot once again, "More?"

I glanced at my full cup, shook my head, and said. "Let's cut to the chase. How long have I been your customer?"

"I'd have to look it up. You tell me."

"At least twenty-five years, probably more."

He nodded.

"And in all this time, have I ever defaulted or failed to meet a financial obligation?"

He shook his head. "Never."

"So, based on my record, how much will you advance me on a line of credit?"

"Jim Bob, you don't want to do this."

"How much?"

He mumbled something, his voice so low I couldn't hear.

"Say again?"

"Maybe $50,000, but I'll have to take it to the loan committee."

"When will I know?" I asked.

CHAPTER 27

The Pen by Our Barn

It was a dull, overcast morning, four days before Christmas, temperature in the low forties. The Potter County Chief Deputy called. I knew he was coming, and I had already explained it all to Liz.

Still, when the sheriff's car pulled into our driveway accompanied by a pickup and horse trailer from the West Texas Stable, it was a heart-wrenching experience. I put my arm around my daughter and held her close. "It's only for a few days," I said, trying my best to stay positive.

"But we don't know for sure, do we?" The tragic uncertainty of her expression broke my heart.

"Nothing's for sure," I replied. But as the words came out of my mouth, I regretted them. In our family, that exact phrase was almost always used in conjunction with leukemia. While the prognosis looked better for Liz, we didn't know *for sure*, so we tried not to talk about it.

Liz and I went over to talk with the deputy and the pickup driver. "Where are you taking him?"

"West Texas Horse Stable," the pickup driver answered as he finished loading Orphan into his trailer.

"Where's that?"

"We're on FM 2219, two and a half miles west of I-27."

"Who'll take responsibility for feeding and exercise?"

"I will. And my wife, Tommie."

I could see a wall of resentment in Liz's eyes and interrupted. "Honey, I've known Tim and Tommie for years. We're lucky to have them taking care of Orphan."

The driver smiled, a look of relief. "Would you like a card?"

"Yes, please," Liz answered.

West Texas Stable

Horse Care & Breeding
Tim & Tommie Dye, Owners

19131 FM Road2219   stable 505-555-1234
Amarillo, TX 79124   cell 505-555-4321

"You're welcome to come see him anytime, Tim said. His business finished, he shook our hands, and drove away.

The deputy took his leave, too, and we watched them drive to the blacktop, turn left, and head south. Liz's facial expression was grim. I could see that we needed to find something to take her mind off of Orphan's move.

"I'd like you to go with us to the airport," I said. "Your grandmother will expect you to be leading the welcoming committee."

"Sure." Liz gave me her *I know what you're up to* smile. "You want me to deflect the sparks that fly when you two get together."

"Not true."

"Mom says that twenty-eight years ago Grandma tried to block your marriage and that you've been fighting ever since."

"I can't believe your mother would say such a thing."

"Dad, I've got eyes."

"Then you can see that I've won her over and that she now has a special place in her heart for Texas, for cattle, and for her son-in-law."

Liz laughed. "Yeah, I know that special place. It starts with an H. . .."

Maggie called from the back porch, interrupting our banter, "Time to go."

I looked at my watch. "Her plane isn't scheduled to arrive for two hours."

Liz interrupted, "Mom wants to take the Buick to the carwash before we go to the airport."

I shook my head. "The inspector general—"

"Come on, Dad, it's no big thing, and if it makes Grandma happy—"

"You have your room ready for inspection?"

"Of course."

I thought about the thousand or more times I'd complained about my daughter's messy room. Grudgingly, I had to admit, my mother-in-law was a genius at intimidation.

"How much have you told your grandmother about Orphan?"

"Zip. I haven't told her anything."

"Why's that?"

"Dad, you don't have to ask."

117

"Humor me. Why don't you discuss your horse with your grand-mother?"

"Well, for one thing, horses defecate," she paused for a moment, "and sometimes it happens in places where it has to be cleaned up."

"So?"

"So when one has a fastidious grandmother, one doesn't go looking for topics that lead to unpleasant truths, which could lead to either discord or possible arguments."

"Coward."

"And I'm her favorite grandchild."

"You're her *only* grandchild."

"And who comes to me when they want someone to handle her?"

"I surrender." I raised my hands, palms out. "I admit, you're the champ when it comes to winning favor with your grandmother."

When we walked up to the car, Maggie held out the keys. "You drive."

The three of us piled into her Buick LeSabre, drove to the Sooper Carwash, and paid for "The Works," their most expensive and thorough cleaning. Thirty minutes later, with a heavy "new car" aroma wafting around us, we drove to the airport.

My mother-in-law looked spectacular when she came through security. Dressed to the nines in Fifth Avenue's finest, she hugged and kissed Maggie and Liz. Then she turned to me and held out her hand.

I shook it.

CHAPTER 28

First Presbyterian Church, Amarillo

Liz sang "O Holy Night" at the Christmas Eve service.

It was the twentieth time she had done so in the past twenty-one years. The tradition started—as so many do—by accident. When Liz was in the first grade, the Bushland Elementary music teacher taught the song to our daughter and featured her on the school's Christmas Program. Liz wowed everyone. This tiny little girl with the big voice, one of the smallest children in the first grade, belted out the song in big beautiful tones that filled the auditorium. The church choir director heard about it and asked Liz to sing it at our church. It was such a hit that he asked her back the following year, and the next, until, Christmas after Christmas, it became a tradition. The minister told me some people came to the midnight service just to hear Liz sing.

A year ago, when illness broke the tradition and our daughter's future looked so uncertain, her absence brought the stark reality of cancer to all the members of our church.

This year, the fact that she could once again sing the familiar song at our traditional service, brought special meaning to Christmas, to our church, and especially, to our family. As the melody wafted out over the packed congregation, Maggie and her mother teared up. I tried not to, but despite my best efforts, I couldn't hold back the emotion. Maggie handed me a Kleenex. Tears of joy can be a release. In this case we had so much to be thankful for . . . it felt wonderful.

Christmas dinner was the best I could remember. The four of us pigged out. Maggie made two pies—pumpkin and pecan. Even Katherine was in a festive mood. She couldn't find anything to complain about.

Late that afternoon, when it appeared the Dallas Cowboys had the game won, Liz asked to drive over to see Orphan. Katherine, true to her nosy nature, wanted to come along to see what her granddaughter was so interested in. Maggie decided to make it a foursome.

I called ahead and, even on Christmas Day, Tommie Dye came out to greet us. She rolled back the full-sized barn door and led the way down a wide, dirt-floored corridor with horse stalls on both sides. I estimated fifty or more compartments, each with half-doors and most with a horse's head sticking out.

"Whew, this place smells," Katherine said.

"Yes, Grandma," Liz answered. "It smells like a barn."

I thought the stables remarkably clean and started to comment, then thought better of it. Why provoke my mother-in-law?

"I can't believe my granddaughter would want to come to a place that smells like—"

"Horseshit," Liz interjected.

"Liz, please," Maggie said.

"Why not call it what it is?" Katherine asked, her eyes carefully inspecting the floor to be vigilant where she stepped.

A horse whinny interrupted.

"There he is," Liz yelled. She ran ahead several stalls and kissed the horse on the nose.

"Yuck," Katherine said.

Orphan nodded his head, nuzzling Liz.

"He looks pleased to see you," I said.

From her pocket, Liz took a small zip-lock plastic bag filled with apple slices. "See what I've brought you?"

We watched as Liz offered slice after slice. She rubbed Orphan's nose and talked to him in a whisper. My heart warmed to see Liz so utterly happy.

Maggie stood by my side, her arm entwined in mine. It was a special moment between us, one I wouldn't have traded for the world.

Katherine looked at her watch.

Tommie made her way to Liz, and they talked about Orphan's exercise.

"I'll wait in the car," Katherine said. She turned and started back, her head up and walking briskly. She had only gone a short way when she stepped in a big pile of horse manure.

I had to turn away to keep from laughing.

Maggie joined her mother and they walked on, carefully.

I waited.

After a few minutes, Liz said her goodbyes and we meandered toward the car.

"Tell me about the auction," she said.

"Not much to say."

"Where?"

"Right here. Probably on the south side of the barn."

"When?"

"Two weeks from today, January 8."

"And we're going to bid?" her voice was hopeful.

"You betcha," I said. "We have a letter of credit from the bank."

"You have any idea how much Orphan will sell for?"

"The folks at the American Quarter Horse Association have said he should bring at least $20,000. Our lawyer, Suzanne McDonald, thinks it may be twice that much."

Her brow crinkled. "You said we have a letter from the bank?"

"Yes."

"How much?"

"Fifty thousand dollars."

We walked on in silence. On the twenty-minute drive home, I noticed that our nice clean car now reeked with the heavy smell of horse manure. No one mentioned it.

CHAPTER 29

At Home on Our ranch

Wednesday, December 26, it snowed—twenty-two inches. More in one day than we'd received in the past five years, combined. With winds out of the north gusting as high as fifty miles per hour, the weather bureau called it "a blizzard." I bundled up, went out to check on my cattle, and found them huddled together on the south side of the barn. The weatherman was right . . . this was a blizzard . . . the worst I'd seen in my forty-something years in Texas.

Rick Husband Amarillo International Airport closed.

Katherine complained because they had canceled her flight.

I put chains on all four wheels of my Chevy Suburban, and drove to the clinic in four-wheel drive, bulldozing my way through piles of white—probably the only vet in the Texas Panhandle who went to his office on a day that set records for snowdrifts. On the other hand, I was absolutely the only vet in the country looking for a way to escape a world-class complainer who'd missed her flight to New York City.

By evening, the snow quit, the winds died, and the Texas State

Highway Department opened I-40 to normal traffic. I drove home in relative ease to find Maggie had fixed a turkey tetrazzini casserole to go with leftover pumpkin and pecan pie. Liz helped me carry in two armloads of piñon and we built a roaring fire. The day ended with the four of us sitting in front of the fireplace drinking eggnog spiked with rum and sprinkled with nutmeg.

As so often happens after a front blows in, the next day dawned with a beautiful clear blue sky, brilliant sunshine, and no wind. American Airlines announced a return to normal operations. Maggie and Liz took Katherine to the airport. I drove to the Potter County Sheriff's Office to inquire about Orphan's auction. An attractive young woman—wearing the standard brown and tan deputy's uniform, and who looked to be about the age of my daughter—met me at the front counter.

"I'd like to register for your sale of the horse that's being sold on January 8."

With a cordial smile, she placed a clipboard on the counter. "Sign here," she said, "and I'll need to see a photo ID and a letter of credit from your bank."

I pulled out my driver's license and handed it to her along with my letter from the Texas State Bank. She took my stuff to a nearby Xerox machine, and I picked up the pen to sign my name.

Two people had already signed. I scribbled my name on line three, and took a moment to see who else had registered.

Line number one was difficult to read. I guessed it to be John Paul Brown or something similar.

Line number two was Edgar Payne, certainly no surprise.

The deputy returned my documents and handed me a stack of instruction material. "If you have a minute, I'd be happy to talk you through the process and see if you have any questions."

"Yes, please."

She pointed to the top sheet. "The sale is a week from Tuesday. It'll be held at West Texas Stables. This information sheet gives the time, place, and procedures." She turned over the top page, and I could see that the second was a map. "This is a map of the Amarillo area and shows the sale location."

"I know where it is."

The third sheet was white card stock with a huge number "3" in bright red. The card was eight and a half by eleven inches, and the number was at least six inches high. It could easily be read a block away.

"This is your bidding card," she said. "When you want to make a bid you hold up the card and say the amount of your bid. Only registered bidders, those with cards, are allowed to make bids."

"Are you the person who'll conduct the sale?"

She smiled and shook her head. "No, that'll be the chief deputy, Joe Richardson."

"Could you talk me through it?" I asked. "This is my first time to bid at a Sheriff's Sale."

"Sure. First, he'll ask to see all the cards so he'll know who's bidding. Then he'll announce a number, a fairly high price that he hopes the horse will sell for, and ask if there are any bids. If no one bids, then he'll pick a lower price and ask. He may go down several times before someone places a bid."

"And when someone bids?"

"We're off. He'll take that number and see if another person will bid more—which almost always happens."

"How does the sale end?"

"He'll always ask three times. When it appears no one will raise the bid, he'll say, 'Going once . . . going twice . . . sold to bidder number three for a million dollars.'"

I smiled at her outrageous sales figure. "Hope you have the wrong price."

She chuckled. "You get the idea. Then, if you're the winning bidder, he'll ask for your personal check in that amount."

"A personal check?"

"Yes, that's to temporarily hold the sale. Then you have four hours to go to your bank and secure a cashier's check."

"So a few hours later I come back with my cashier's check and a horse trailer?"

"And we give you your horse and his papers."

I thanked her for her information and drove back to the office. My secretary, Ida Mae, handed me a stack of pink slips—telephone calls for me to return. "I put Paul's slip on top," she said. "He sounded pretty insistent about seeing you today."

I looked down to see the name Paul Edwards and his phone number. "What's up?"

"He didn't say."

I called and got Paul's secretary.

"Mr. Edwards is out in the feed yard," she said. "He wants to know if you could meet him for lunch today at the Big Texan Steakhouse."

"Sure. What time?"

"Would twelve o'clock work for you?"

I said yes, and she signed off. Still no hint of what the cattleman wanted to see me about.

I finished my pink slips, made two appointments for the following day, and left the office a few minutes before noon to drive to the restaurant. When I got there I found Paul sitting at a table by the window.

"How's the snow in Sagebrush?" I asked.

"Starting to melt," he replied. "Couple of days like today, and it'll be gone."

"You lose any cattle?" I asked.

"Not that I know of," he replied. "These short-lived snowstorms don't seem to bother cattle feeding operations."

"How many head you feeding?"

He smiled. "That a rhetorical question?"

"Hey, I'm not trying to be nosy."

"You know our capacity is 490,000. Let's just say that we're slightly under that limit at the present time."

"But still the largest in the country?"

"Probably."

The waitress came and took our orders.

She left and I turned to Paul. "What's happening?" I asked.

He held up a sheet of white card stock with the number "4" in bright red. The card looked exactly like mine except that it was one digit different. A wave of fear rippled down my spine.

There was no way I could bid against this billionaire cattleman.

Chapter 30

The Big Texan Steakhouse, Amarillo

"Relax," Paul said, "I'm not going to enter the bidding against you."

"That number?" I nodded toward his card with the big red "4."

The waitress brought our drinks.

"I'm signed up as your insurance policy," he said.

"Insurance?"

"What's your top bid?" he asked.

"I have a letter of credit from my bank in the amount of $50,000."

"What'll you do if someone—say Edgar Payne—bids higher?"

"I talked with a trainer, a guy named Gus Gonzalez, who is very knowledgeable about the racing business. He told me the horse shouldn't sell for more than $20,000."

"Ever been to an auction for racehorses?"

"No."

"Sometimes they sell for more than they're worth," Paul said. "Last September, at the big sale in Ruidoso, I saw a horse sell for

$500,000."

"Wow, a half-million?"

"The chances that horse will ever pay out are infinitesimal. Even if he won the All American Futurity, he wouldn't be worth that price."

"Why would anyone pay more than a horse is worth?"

"Good question, but the facts show us, in the horse business, people often do."

"So you're thinking someone—someone like Edgar Payne—could, for spurious reasons, make an artificially high bid for Orphan?"

"It happens."

"And if he does?"

"I might make a contest of it."

"Paul."

"You saved my business once, Jim Bob."

"That was different."

"Suppose American beef production had gone down like the British market did?"

"But it didn't."

"Yes, thanks to you."

The waitress brought our food—two large hamburgers with french fries. Paul asked for catsup and more coffee. I waited while she tended to his requests, feeling grateful for a moment to gather my thoughts.

When the waitress left, I said, "Paul, I appreciate your good intentions." I watched as he upended a red bottle and flooded his plate.

"What're friends for?" He speared a fork-full of potatoes

slathered in catsup.

I left my food untouched. "This is more than friendship. We're talking about the possibility of big bucks."

"Doesn't matter—you can pay me back." He picked up his hamburger with both hands and took a big bite.

"That's just the point," I replied. "There's a good reason why the bank limited my letter to $50,000."

When he swallowed and cleared his mouth, he gestured to my plate. "Wish you'd eat. Makes me nervous when I'm paying for lunch and you won't touch it."

"This makes me more than nervous," I replied. "It scares the hell out of me."

"Food scares you?"

"Cut it out. You know what I mean."

He stopped eating and slouched back in his chair. "I'm just trying to help a friend."

"I know you are, and I appreciate it—more than you can possibly understand."

"But?"

"But I can't let you bid on this horse at a figure that'll take me into bankruptcy."

"I told you, we can work it out—later."

"Paul, please."

He looked away. The two of us sat silently for several moments.

"What is it you want me to do?" he asked.

"Stay out of it."

He rolled his eyes. "Jim Bob, you are the stubbornest sonvabitch in West Texas. You wouldn't recognize a gift horse if he licked you on the mouth."

"I think the word is looked—if he *looked* you in the mouth." I picked up my hamburger and took a bite.

"What about your daughter?" He took another bite of catsup-laden potatoes.

"She'll be okay. She understands life has its limitations."

We finished our lunch in silence. Paul paid. I thanked him as best I could. We parted as friends, but with a firm understanding about the auction.

That afternoon I made rounds at two big feed yards in Deaf Smith County. It felt good to be treating animals, to be helping cattlemen, to be in control of my work.

Driving home I tried to think of a way to be in control of a horse.

CHAPTER 31

At Home on Our Ranch in Bushland, Texas

Over the next eleven days a thickening cloud of uncertainty gathered over our home. Liz moped around with little to occupy her time. I went to work, but when I returned Maggie related to me the details of how Liz would try to practice her singing, become frustrated, and go out to the empty barn where she lingered for hours. On the weekend before the auction, I worked at home and observed personally her symptoms of depression.

Sunday night, after we'd gone to bed, Maggie and I talked into the night and finally decided we needed to hold a frank discussion with our daughter. We agreed the best time would be at the next morning at breakfast. I tossed and turned the rest of the night, sleeping fitfully, dreading the morning.

Maggie mixed batter for Belgian waffles, Liz's favorite. She had it ready for our usual seven o'clock breakfast. I read and re-read the paper.

We waited. Eight o'clock came and went. I called the office and told them I'd be coming in late.

Nine o'clock came. Finally, Maggie awakened Liz and told her we wanted to talk.

I sat at the kitchen table and listened to the shower running. Maggie fried sausage and started the waffle iron.

Liz came to the table. "What is this? The Inquisition?"

"The auction's tomorrow," I replied.

"Oh, really?" Liz's voice dripped with sarcasm.

"We thought it would be good to discuss it as a family."

"What's there to discuss?" She slipped into a chair, her mouth set in a hard line of frustration and ire.

I tried to think of how best to meet her negative outlook.

Maggie brought a stack of waffles and a plate of sausage to the table. It smelled wonderful.

"We can talk about all of the possible outcomes," I continued, "and our plans for how we'll respond to each."

Liz stabbed a waffle and a couple of sausage patties, then doused them with warm maple syrup. "Dad?"

"Yes."

"We all know that thug, the infamous Mr. Payne, is going to out-bid us. There's nothing left to discuss."

"What if he doesn't?" I continued.

"You told me he made a vow after the trial. He swore he would do whatever it took to get Orphan."

"That's true, but it doesn't necessarily mean it will happen. Sometimes, when people are upset, they make empty threats."

Maggie interrupted, "I remember a little girl who threatened to run away from home when she was five years old because her mother wouldn't let her chew three sticks of bubble gum when she went to bed."

Liz took a bite of waffle. After she chewed and swallowed, she took a long draw of milk. She looked at her mother, then at me. "You're saying the evil Mr. Payne made a childish threat?"

"Words are words," I replied. "But when it comes to money, reality has a way of forcing a person's decisions."

Liz reached for more syrup. "So you think we still have a chance?"

"A very good chance, but if we pay top dollar for a race horse, we're going to have to race him."

"I'll bet Orphan would love that." Liz took another forkful of waffle.

"Suzie, our lawyer, talked with me about a trainer named Gus Gonzalez. He runs a stable down on Hunsley Road. She says he's reputed to be the finest trainer in this area. He's had several horses who've won the All American."

Liz set her fork on her plate alongside her half-eaten waffle. "I have a request."

Maggie and I stopped eating and looked at her.

"Okay," I replied.

"Let's not make any big plans."

"Fine with me," I said.

Maggie cleared her throat. "And I have a request."

"Okay," I said, again.

"I'd like us to discuss what we're going to do if Payne or somebody else outbids us."

A red light went on in my brain, and I thought about the night almost eight months ago when Liz's GvHD symptoms first appeared. My thoughtless remarks about losing Orphan probably had nothing to do with her illness. She had the disease. Yet, the fact that her symptoms erupted coincidentally with my remarks about getting another horse signaled me to be cautious.

"First, let me say that there's considerable evidence that Payne may be crazy. He's done several irrational things when I've been around him."

Neither Liz nor Maggie offered a response.

"Second, I think $50,000 will be more than enough to win the bid."

"Even against a crazy?" Liz asked.

"Yes," I continued. "And when we own Orphan, he'll be a two-year-old and ready to go to a trainer like Gus Gonzalez."

"Dad." Liz's impatience was rising to the surface again.

"Hear me out?" I pleaded. "I'm trying to make the point, win or lose, Orphan is no longer going to be the same. We'll no longer have a baby horse we can treat as a pet."

"So your point is?" Liz asked.

"That even if we win the bid, we'll have to send him away to a trainer. It's time to prepare him for racing."

For a moment, none of us spoke. Then Liz picked up her fork and took a bite of waffle.

So did Maggie.

I did the same, and for a few moments we chewed silently.

Liz spoke first, "If we don't get him," she said, a quiver in her voice, "I hope it's Paul Jones or one of the big-time stables, so Orphan will have the training he needs to win races." She looked away, but not before I could see moisture in her eyes.

"Anyone except Payne," Maggie added.

In my heart of hearts, I truly thought we would have the winning bid. I started to say it again, but I thought about Liz's comment. She hoped, if we didn't get Orphan, he would go to a big-name, professional racing stable.

Maybe that would be best.

CHAPTER 32

The West Texas Horse Stable

We got there early. And the size of the crowd surprised me.

The sign-up sheet for Orphan's auction showed twenty-six bidders.

Uniformed sheriff's deputies were roaming around everywhere, the most I'd ever seen at one place.

Representatives from the American Quarter Horse Association swelled the turnout. The *AQHA Journal* interviewed me and took a photo of Liz with Orphan.

About an hour before auction time, the media gathered in full force. All three Amarillo TV stations sent remote trucks with their tall, aerial antennas, reporters, and camera crews. The *Amarillo Globe-News* sent both a reporter and a photographer. KGNC radio set up for a remote broadcast. Even the WTAMU student newspaper had a representative. The worst part was the number of people who wanted to photograph and interview me. At first I was flattered, but the endless repetition quickly got old, and I tried to find a way to duck their requests.

Suzanne McDonald helped me.

"What're you doing here, Suzie?" I asked.

"If you have to ask, then I don't think you'd understand if I told you."

"Have you seen the list of bidders?"

She pulled out a clipboard with all twenty-six names, their addresses, and their company. She started down the list.

"Johnny Jones owns the leading stable in Oklahoma. This past year he had three horses in the All American. He's a serious bidder."

"Wow." I had expected to tell her about the twenty-six bidders. She was a mile ahead of me.

"Number two is Payne, you're number three, and Paul Edwards is four."

"Paul has agreed to lay out." I watched her face.

Her reaction was to read the next name. "Number five is Betty Walker, a widow who lives in Canyon. She'll bid $25,000 tops."

"How do you know?"

She raised her eyebrows in a Groucho Marx gesture, ignoring my question, and went on with her list. "Numbers six and seven are local farmers looking for a bargain. They're not serious contenders."

We moved aside, turning our backs to avoid a television reporter and cameraman. Suzie continued, "Number eight is from Kentucky. He won the Triple Crown last year and is reported to be interested in building a successful quarter-horse stable. He probably has big bucks."

She continued on down the list, giving a thumbnail summary of each. Her research amazed me with its detail and analysis.

"I thought you said this auction would be too little and too late—that no one would be here to compete?"

"Not the first time I've been wrong," she replied, her expression somber.

"Looks like we're dead in the water before it even starts."

"One never knows. Remember Yogi Berra's famous line?"

"It ain't over 'til it's over?"

She smiled, a brief acknowledgement of my quote, then changed the subject, "What's your top bid?" she asked.

"My letter says $50,000."

"That might do it. Are you prepared to put all of it on the line?"

"Yes, but that's my limit. I can't go any higher."

The flow of the crowd shifted, moving outside the barn. She looked at her watch. "Showtime."

We walked around to the south side of the building where I estimated a hundred or more people had gathered. We found Liz and Maggie standing in the front row and squeezed in beside them.

The chief deputy and his assistant—the young woman I remembered from the sign-up counter—stood in front of a mike and started the auction. He began by calling numbers. When he said "three," I held up my card. As he went through the list, we watched with interest and learned that only nineteen of the twenty-six bidders were present. It amazed me that seven had dropped out. I thought about making it eight.

"We'll open the bidding at $50,000," the auctioneer said. "Will anyone give fifty thousand for this horse?"

No one bid.

"How about $40,000? Do I hear forty?"

No takers.

"I'll take a bid of $30,000."

Silence.

"Let's start at $25,000. Is there someone who'll give twenty-five?" He looked around the crowd.

"I'll bid $20,000," said Edgar Payne, holding up his card. He stood about fifteen feet to my right, near the end of the front row.

"We have a bid of $20,000 from number two," the auctioneer called.

"I'll give $30,000," said a voice from the back.

"We have $30,000 from number fourteen."

"Thirty-five," Payne said.

"Forty," came a different voice from the back.

The auctioneer's voice came over the PA system. "We have a bid of $40,000 from number twenty-six."

"Forty-five," Payne called, his voice loud, a scowl on his face.

Suzie punched me lightly. "Now or never."

"I held up my big red three, $50,000," I said, my voice shaky.

The auctioneer repeated my bid and my number over his PA.

I held my breath for the next few moments.

"We have $50,000," the auctioneer said.

"Fifty-five," Payne said. He turned to stare straight at me. People near me stepped back.

"We now have $55,000 from number two," the auctioneer said, his voice booming over the PA.

Again, a quiet came over the crowd.

"We have $55,000, do I hear more?"

We waited.

"Going once for $55,000."

A momentary pause.

"Going twice for—"

"Seventy-five thousand," said a familiar voice from behind me.

I turned to see Paul Edwards holding up his card.

"From number four we have a bid of $75,000," repeated the auctioneer over his PA. The crowd shifted with renewed energy. People strained to see the new bidder.

I heard cursing from my right. Several people moved, trying to distance themselves from the outburst of profanity. I was learning to develop an understanding—an expectation—of Edgar Payne. Obviously, he had a wild, uncontrollable temper. I had seen him boil over at Anna Garcia, and then again explode a year later outside the courtroom. His behavior now loomed as a threat to the auction, and I wondered how it could continue.

The auctioneer chastised him, referring to the rules of decorum published in the information packet we had each received. Four deputies came and stood at the end of the row, less than ten feet from Payne.

A silence fell over the crowd. No one moved. I had the feeling of time standing still.

At least a full minute passed before the announcer moved. Finally, he spoke, his lips close to the microphone. "We have a bid of $75,000. Do I hear more?"

Nothing.

"Going once."

The tension abated.

"Going twice."

I could feel a sense of release in myself, and I thought, throughout the gathering.

It was short-lived.

"I bid $76,000," Payne said, holding up his card.

The crowd came alive. People standing near me whispered. I

looked over my shoulder to witness the animated reaction of virtually every person at the auction.

"Whoa," Suzie whispered.

Even the auctioneer acted surprised. He paused, turned, and said something to his assistant. She nodded. "I believe we have a bid for $76,000 from number two. Is that right, sir?"

"God damned right," Payne yelled.

"Sir, I must remind you that our rules specify no profanity. If you refuse to abide by the published auction procedures, you'll be disqualified and escorted from the property."

"You gonna accept my bid or not?" Payne snarled, his face twisted in anger.

Before the auctioneer could respond, another bid came from behind me.

"One hundred thousand," said Paul Edwards.

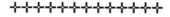

The crowd dispersed.

Liz, Maggie, and I lingered to watch Paul write a personal check and leave it with the chief deputy. I glanced at my wife and daughter, their faces somber. Liz, especially, looked as though she were attending a funeral, the loss of a family member.

"Congratulations," I said, though I didn't feel it, trying to convey an upbeat emotion, a sense of well-wishes for a friend.

"You got a minute?" Paul asked.

I nodded.

"I'd like you to go with me to the bank to get a cashier's check," he said. "I can give you a ride home."

I gave the keys to the Suburban to Maggie. Paul and I climbed into his pickup and headed toward his bank in downtown Amarillo.

I laughed. "You dirty, lying, sonovabitch, you promised to stay out of this," I said as we drove north on I-27.

"Hey, I tried."

"Not hard enough."

"You wanted me to hold back and let Payne have the horse?"

"There was no need to jump the bid to $100,000."

"So you say."

"It seemed obvious that Payne was stretching to raise your last bid."

"Dr. Masterson, friend, you're an expert in veterinary medicine. People have told me that someday you'll receive the Nobel Prize for your testing of BSE."

I could hear it coming.

"Why do you find it so hard to admit," he continued, "that I might know more than you about horse trading?"

He had me. He was right, and we both knew it. A few minutes later we drove into Bank of America's parking garage, took the stairs down into the tunnel, walked under Eighth Street to the lobby, and rode the elevator up to the second floor. This surprised me. I thought we'd go to a teller's window on the first floor to get a cashier's check, but, as I learned that morning, the very rich have a different way of doing their banking. We went to the executive suite.

"Good morning, Mr. Edwards," the secretary said with a bright smile as she picked up the phone. "I'll tell him you're here."

A moment later, the door opened and the bank's executive vice president came out. Paul introduced me, and we followed him into a lavishly furnished office where the secretary served us coffee.

"As expected, I bought the horse and need a cashier's check," Paul said.

"How much?" the banker asked.

"Make a guess," Paul replied.

The banker sipped his coffee and looked down to open a file folder on his desk. "I see you had asked for a million-dollar line of credit. I'll bet you bought him for half that much—$500,000."

Paul laughed. "You missed it by a few dollars. Make the check for $100,000."

"Payable to the Potter County Sheriff's Sale?"

"Yup."

The banker picked up his phone and ordered the check.

That morning I learned something else about the super rich—there's no waiting around to get money. By the time I'd finished my coffee, the secretary returned with the check and a paper for Paul to sign. In less than fifteen minutes, we were in-and-out, and headed south on I-27.

"I need some place to keep this horse," Paul said. "I'll pay a hundred dollars a day."

In the back of my mind I kind of expected this was coming, but I had to ask the question anyway. "Why do you want me to keep Orphan?"

"He's an expensive horse. I can't take him to any old stable for boarding. He needs the special care that only people like you and your daughter will provide."

"That's horseshit, and you know it," I said, beginning to grin.

"The question is, will you do it?"

"Sure, but not for a hundred dollars a day."

"You want more?"

I laughed. "You and I both know dozens of stables where the going rate is twenty-five dollars per day. If it's only temporary, I'll do it for friendship."

"You don't get it, do you?"

I shook my head. "Get what?"

"Several things. First, everyone knows it costs more to board an expensive racehorse than an old nag that's just a family pet. Second, we need to establish a 'going rate' so when you submit your bill to the sheriff you have a figure you can quote."

I thought about what he was saying. The light dawned.

"How long have you been boarding the horse?" Paul asked.

"Almost two years to the day," I replied.

"How much is 730 days at a hundred dollars per day?"

I did the easy math. "That's $73,000."

"Plus a couple thousand for veterinary services and your fee for hauling him from the wreck to your place. I think you should round it to $76,000."

Taken aback, I said, "I'd feel like a horse thief if I charged that much."

"Jim Bob," he snorted. "The sheriff is expecting to pay. It's in the judge's orders."

"Not that much. A hundred dollars a day is exorbitant."

"Trust me. He'll be glad to pay it, because it leaves him a profit of nearly $25,000, and it clears his books."

"I don't know—" It didn't sound right to me.

"Orphan's for sale," he said. "You interested?"

"I can't afford him."

"The price is $101,000." He smiled.

Before I could answer, we arrived back at the West Texas Stables where we found the chief deputy. Paul gave him his check, and at Paul's insistence, I wrote out a bill in the amount of $76,000 for boarding the horse, for transportation, and for vet services. The chief deputy took it without comment.

Later that day, an ecstatic Liz and I picked up Orphan and took him home.

Three weeks later, we received a check from the Potter County Sheriff's Office in the amount of $76,000.

CHAPTER 33

West Texas Horse Stable

On the first Monday in February, Paul Edwards called—early—while Maggie, Liz, and I were still seated around the kitchen table having breakfast. He asked if he could stop by for some horse trading.

"When?" I asked.

"Fifteen minutes," he said.

We finished our breakfast just as Paul's white Ford pickup passed the kitchen window and came to a halt out by the barn. Liz and I put on our coats and went out to meet him.

"How's my horse? Paul asked as he walked toward the fence.

"Just fine," Liz answered. She and I hurried to catch up.

Liz went in to feed Orphan. Paul and I stopped at the fence to watch.

"It's time for me to sell him," Paul said.

"How much?" I asked.

"Hasn't changed—$101,000."

"You might get more if you advertised," I suggested, "or listed him on the Internet."

"Hey, you big nincompoop. The reason I bought this horse was to sell him to you."

I'd always thought that was the case, but until that moment—until he looked at me and actually said the words—I'd never been sure. I hesitated for a moment, trying to organize my thoughts and find a way to express my gratitude.

Paul didn't wait. "I'm looking to sell him this morning," he said. "You interested?"

"Of course."

And then—a gesture that hit me like a lightning bolt—Paul stuck out his hand. "Deal?"

When someone holds out his hand, I can't seem to ignore it without appearing rude. So I shook it.

"You got any coffee?" he asked.

With my mind still reeling, I struggled to answer. "We can probably find some in the kitchen," I mumbled.

He slapped me playfully on the back, and we walked together up to the house where Maggie already had a fresh pot brewing. I pulled the checkbook from our family "financial" drawer by the phone.

Paul and I sat. Maggie poured three cups and joined us.

With a shaky hand, it took me three tries to write the check. The first time I wrote one hundred and one dollars. Seeing it was wrong, I tore up the check and started over, but couldn't get it to fit in the space. The third time, using tiny letters, I got it right and handed the check to Paul. "It's the largest check I've ever written."

"And one of the best," Paul replied.

"Only time will tell," Maggie added with a worried look.

Paul finished his coffee, stuffed the check in his shirt pocket, and left with a big smile.

I called the office and took the day off.

Liz and I drove toward Gus Gonzalez's training stables located on Hunsley Road, about ten miles south of Amarillo. For a big-time trainer, he displayed a very small business sign, and it took a couple of passes before we spotted it.

The buildings were set back from the road, about a quarter-mile. As we drove north on a narrow gravel lane to his home, I understood why. What at first had looked like an empty pasture turned out to be an enormous oval, a racetrack.

We found several pickups and horse trailers in the parking lot behind the house. I left the Suburban alongside the other vehicles. About a hundred yards away from the next building, sat a huge red barn. Inside, my impression of Gonzalez Training Stable changed dramatically. What had first appeared, from our drive-by on Hunsley Road, to be a very modest rural residence, was now revealed as an enormous, professional horse training center. As far as the eye could see were horse stalls, meticulously kept, each with the traditional half-door and most with a large net of hay hanging nearby.

Halfway down the corridor we found an office, and Gus talking on the phone. He waved us in. While we waited I looked around the room at an impressive collection of horseracing memorabilia. Every square inch of wall space was covered with plaques, certificates, and photographs. At the end of the room stood a glass display case crammed with trophies. Most had a horse, horse's head, or jockey on top.

Gus finished his conversation and walked out from behind his desk, and shook hands, and exchanged pleasantries.

While we were talking, a young Hispanic man in riding clothes came to the door. "Everything's ready," he said.

"We're set up to do a breeze," Gus said. "Wanna watch?"

Liz and I nodded. We followed Gus and his rider out of the barn to a fence by the racetrack where we found another rider, a young woman, and the two horses. Gus explained to us that the word "breeze" is a term used by horse trainers to describe an easy race, part of the training for young horses. Gus' usual, step-by-step training consisted of a number of races where the objective was to show a young horse just what it was like to compete.

Liz and I watched as Gus loaded the two horses into starting gates. When they were ready, he pushed a button, the gates flew open, an electric bell sounded, and the horses took off. What Gus called a breeze, appeared to me as a flat-out race, both horses running as fast as they could.

Then, in just seconds, it was all over. At the far end of the field, the horses slowed, turned, and started walking back.

"That was quick," Liz said.

"Have you attended many quarter horse races?" Gus asked.

"I guess that was my first." She smiled at the admission.

"Most are only a quarter-mile," he continued. "Do you know how long it takes a top-notch horse to run it?"

Liz shook her head. "Not really."

"Usually twenty-one or twenty-two seconds."

That was news to me, and I began to realize how little I knew about horseracing in general and quarter horseracing in particular.

Gus pointed to the barn, and we followed him toward it.

"Tell me about your horse," he said. "I've heard he has expensive bloodlines."

I gave him a copy of the AQHA registration papers.

We stopped for a moment while Gus scanned the documents with an experienced eye. "Wow," he said as he handed them back. "Looks like you've got yourself a heck of a horse. Let's go do some serious talk about training."

On the way we found the grooms spraying the horses—what Gus called *a bath*. We stopped to look.

"After the bath we take them out to the walker," he explained.

"What's a walker?" Liz asked.

"I'll show you," he replied.

We followed Gus, the two horses, and their grooms back outside to a large steel frame shaped like a giant umbrella. The contraption was at least thirty feet in diameter and powered by a small electric motor. A path that matched the exact circumference of the device gave me a clue about its name—the walker.

The grooms attached a lead rope to each of the two horses and then turned on the motor. Slowly it began to rotate like a merry-go-round, and the horses, apparently expecting the drill, began to walk around in a circle.

"You'll find all training facilities have walkers," Gus said. "It's an essential part of horseracing—the cooling off period."

"So you'll hook Orphan up to one of these?" Liz asked.

Gus nodded. "After every race." He started back toward his office. "Let's go talk about our plans."

Liz and I accompanied him back to his office.

"Is Orphan broke?" Gus asked.

"Sorta," Liz replied. "I ride him every day, but so far, I'm the only one who has ridden him."

"Anyone else ever tried?"

Liz shook her head. "Just me."

Gus frowned. "That may be a problem. "Sometimes a one-rider horse is harder to train than one that has never been broken."

"When will we know?" I asked.

"When we put a bit in his mouth, a saddle on his back, and a new rider on top."

I wanted to ask when would be the best time to do this, but Gus took over the conversation. He lectured me about the fact that not all horses with top-notch bloodlines, like Orphan, turn out to be great racehorses.

"And we won't know until we start training?" I asked.

"Exactly."

"When do you want to begin?"

"Tomorrow."

CHAPTER 34

Our Ranch, Bushland, Texas

Tuesday, February 5, was a day I'll always remember. Our baby, who had been living in our barn since he was two weeks old, was leaving us. Liz, especially, reacted with emotion. She fed him—one last time. Then she took him for a ride, a nice easy gallop around the pasture. In the meantime, I hitched up the trailer and backed it around to the gate. When she returned, we loaded him.

Driving south I tried to build conversation.

"Liz, you can visit Orphan as often as you like."

"I know."

"It's only twenty miles."

"I don't want to interfere."

"Talk to Gus."

"I already have." Her voice quivered. "I called him last night."

"What did he say?"

"He said he thought Orphan would do better if I stayed away for a week or two."

"What's a week? He was gone longer for the Sheriff's Sale."

"Yes, and I nearly went crazy."

"What about your singing?"

"Dad."

"Want me to stay out of it?"

"In case you've forgotten, I am twenty-seven-years-old."

"Really?"

She smiled. But we rode the rest of the way in silence.

I backed up to Gus' big red barn. He met us, helped us unload, and asked Liz to ride Orphan around the oval racetrack.

She did.

Gus and I watched.

"Good looking horse," he said. "Nice confirmation."

"What's confirmation?"

He gave me a look that reminded me of my kindergarten teacher. Only he would be thinking, *you're a veterinarian, you should know racehorse lingo.* I thought about saying, *I doctor cattle. Ask me about bovine disease,* but I didn't.

"It's the way the horse is put together," he replied. "It's the shape, especially, the proportion of the muscular structure."

I didn't know what to say in response, so I changed the subject. "Uh, what's the plan?" I asked.

"For training?"

I nodded.

"First, you have to realize you're at least three months behind. All of these other two-year olds," he gestured with a sweep of his arm to indicate the dozens of other horses at his training stable, "have been here since last fall."

"Oh," and I gradually began to see the intensity of the horseracing business.

Gus lectured.

I listened.

He gave me a short course in preparing two-year-olds for horseracing.

First he would have to break Orphan. That could take days or weeks, depending on the horse's personality, and his resistance to human commands.

"You just saw my daughter ride him. Why would you have to spend weeks breaking him?"

Gus responded with a question. "Have we talked about problems with a one-rider horse?"

"A little."

"Orphan could be more difficult to train than one who has never had a bit in his mouth or a saddle on his back."

"I bet it'll go fine," I said. "Orphan's always been a gentle horse."

Gus rolled his eyes. "We'll see."

He moved us and our conversation to a spot over by the round pens. Gus had several, fifty feet in diameter and with solid fences seven feet high. We watched horses at work in each, while he described how, in the wild, horses have a natural instinct to run off in a variety of directions. He made a big deal about the obvious— when a horse enters a race, it must run straight ahead. The round pen was, for most horses, an introduction to running in a prescribed direction, or in this case, running in a circle by the fence. At first this was done with a long lead—a person in the center of the pen holding a twenty-five-foot rope. Later, a rider would run the horse without the rope. Training continued, day after day, until the horse expected to follow the fence.

Once a horse became accustomed to running in a prescribed

direction—responding to the rider's commands—training would move out to the field and eventually to the big oval racetrack. At first, Gus said, the training would be light, an easy lope with occasional starts and stops. As the horse demonstrated responsiveness to commands, the speed would increase and the demands would grow more complex. Gradually the horse would be allowed to run with other horses.

If all went well, Gus hoped Orphan would be ready in ten to twelve weeks to receive "gate training." He lectured me at length about how important this was. In quarter horse racing, the entire race lasts only a little more than twenty seconds. A horse's exit from the gate can be the deciding factor in who wins.

We talked as we walked, eventually ending up at Orphan's stall in the barn. Liz was rubbing his nose and feeding him apple slices.

"I notice Orphan doesn't have a brand," Gus said. "I could do a freeze brand for you."

"We thought the four white socks and the white blaze would be enough to identify him," I replied.

"Chestnut and Sorrel are the two most common quarter horses. I've seen dozens that have white markings like this. It would be smart to add a freeze brand, and I can do it for you."

"Freeze brand?"

"Dry ice. We hold it there for a minute to freeze the horse's skin. When it peels off, the hair will come back white. I suggest you use my WT brand—do it on the hip."

I looked at Liz.

"How much pain?" she asked.

"Not much," Gus replied. "Most horses just stand there. Only takes a minute."

"Okay," I said.

I couldn't see the need for a brand, but I wanted Gus to think of me as agreeable.

CHAPTER 35

At Home in Bushland, Texas

February eased into March, and our family adapted. In a major change from the past two years, I went to work at the veterinary clinic with no thought about any responsibilities for the care and feeding of a horse. Maggie's life didn't shift as much as mine, but I could tell a difference. She now devoted more energy to homemaking and to her volunteer activities, without distractions from the animal that had dominated our family thinking and planning.

Liz was the one most affected.

Because her daily routine had been so intensely focused on Orphan, her new directions were much more noticeable. Now, with the horse gone, she returned to the first great passion of her life—singing. She made arrangements for an accompanist at Amarillo College and started talking about a recital. We still talked about Orphan and, after the first two weeks, she made visits to the Gonzalez Training Stables, but it was obvious in our daily interaction, she was starting to think about returning to New York.

At the dinner table, on Tuesday evening of that first week in

March, she asked about us taking her to the Sloan Kettering Cancer Center for a checkup. Her question alarmed me.

"How are you feeling?" I asked.

"Fine," she replied.

"Any new symptoms?"

She shook her head. "Dad, I just want to go in for a checkup, to see what they think about me trying to restart my singing career. It's been six months."

I thought back to the attack of GvHD—October, November, December, January, February, March—"

"Honey, I think that would be great," Maggie interrupted. "Want me to go with you?"

"Actually, I was hoping all three of us could go, spend a few days, take in an opera."

I felt a shoe strike my ankle and looked up to see Maggie glaring at me.

"Sounds great," I said. "When do you want to go?"

"Next month?" Liz suggested.

Maggie and I agreed. Conversation shifted to the details of trip planning. Liz would make the arrangements and let us know.

The date would remain vividly in my memory because of the wind. The next day it came with a vengeance. It blew from the southwest at forty-five miles per hour, gusting to sixty. With it came the dust—topsoil from the vast desert area between Lubbock and El Paso. Sandy, reddish particles that turned the sky dark. The Texas Panhandle at its worst, I drove home late that afternoon with my lights on.

I put on goggles and walked out into the pasture to check on my small herd of Black Angus. They had gathered on the leeward side of the barn, huddled together away from the wind—all twenty present and accounted for.

Next I checked the windmill. It was locked down in the "off" position, a safety precaution because of the high wind, but the water had become stagnant, the surface covered with dirt, grime, and debris. Wind or no wind, I had to do something. My cattle couldn't drink from a water trough in this condition.

Cautiously, I unlocked the tail blade to swing the windmill into the wind. Using all my strength, I inched the big wheel around until it faced the full force of the gale. At first I didn't know if the pump mechanism could take it, so I kept my hands on the control lever, ready to swing it back to the "stop" position. The wheel spun furiously, driving the pump up-and-down at record speed.

It held.

Water poured into the tank like a fireman's hose. I stayed with it until the water level came up to "overflow" status and the flotsam layer began to drain over the side of the tank. Standing there, braced against the wind, seemed like hours, though it was probably less than thirty minutes. As the sun fell lower in the west, the wind slackened. Finally, after most of the grime had flowed away, I tied down the windmill in the "off" position, walked around the barn to the cattle, and tried to drive them to the water tank.

They didn't want to go.

With the easing of the wind, my yelling and pushing, and their thirst motivating them, eventually they came around to the tank. I headed inside.

"Look at you," Maggie exclaimed, taking me in from head to toe.

We have a small mirror on the wall by the kitchen door. I looked. The raccoon-like image staring back at me was unrecognizable. The area around my eyes, where the goggles had been, was white but the wind had layered the rest of my face with dust, dirt, and grime—so much that it had obliterated my features.

I headed straight for the shower.

A few minutes later I joined Maggie and Liz at the kitchen table for fried chicken, green beans, mashed potatoes, and gravy.

"How's Orphan?" I asked.

"Didn't go today," Liz replied. "Because of the wind, they didn't take any of the horses outside."

"Veterinarians didn't work outside, either," I said.

"The Channel 10 weatherman says the wind will ease tonight," Maggie offered. "He predicts tomorrow will be a beautiful day."

"And I've made arrangements for our trip," Liz said.

"You did? Tell us all about it," Maggie urged.

She did.

In the first week in April, the three of us would take American Airlines to the Big Apple. Liz made an appointment with Dr. Lawrence Strong at Sloan Kettering, arranged a meeting with Robert Van House, the executive director of the Metropolitan Opera, and bought tickets for the three of us to *Das Rheingold*.

We were scheduled to leave on Tuesday, April 8.

CHAPTER 36

At Home in Bushland

It rained a lot in the next few weeks. The dust settled, trees sprouted leaves, the grass began to green, and the Mastersons adjusted to our new, horseless lifestyle. Well, Maggie and I adjusted—and Liz spent more time on singing—but after the first two weeks of Orphan's absence, she made frequent trips to the Gonzalez Training Stables.

Each night at dinner, we discussed two main topics—our upcoming trip to New York and a report on Orphan's progress. The "horse report" usually dominated our conversation.

Orphan's acceptance of new riders had gone well and he was considered "broken" in about seven days. By the time the calendar turned to April, training in the round pen had finished, and he graduated to daily runs on the big, oval racetrack. Maggie and I usually went to see our horse at least once a week.

Because of our trip, we made special arrangements to visit the training stable and see him run. Gus scheduled a time for us to observe a "breeze," a trial run for 350 yards.

So it happened that we were there on the first Monday in April, the day before we were scheduled to fly to New York. The weather cooperated, and at ten o'clock on a beautiful, sunny, spring morning the four of us—Liz, Maggie, Gus, and I—gathered by the track as trainers loaded Orphan and another horse into the starting gate. We stood at the 350-yard marker. Gus held his stopwatch.

The bell rang, the gates burst open, and the two horses came charging down the track. For the next eighteen seconds we watched with excitement until Orphan thundered past us, a full length in front of the other horse.

I thought Orphan looked good.

Liz and Maggie smiled, obviously pleased that our horse came out in front.

Gus' reaction was somber. He stared at his stopwatch, frowning—a puzzled look on his face.

"What's the matter?" I asked.

He showed me the digital readout on his timer and read the numbers aloud as I looked at them, "Seventeen point ninety-four."

"Is that good?" I asked.

"Jim Bob, that is unbelievable. I'm wondering if I accidentally tripped the button late at the start or early at the finish."

"You think it's a false reading?"

"Has to be," he answered, shaking his head. "No horse has ever run 350 yards in less than eighteen seconds."

"Who was that horse he raced against?"

"Midnight Dash. And that's something else that doesn't make sense. She's our fastest horse. In all our training trials, no horse has ever beat her."

Orphan and Midnight walked around the oval, cooling down.

We followed Gus back into the big red barn and waited by his office while he took a phone call. A few minutes later the two riders came in and unsaddled their horses. Grooms took the sweaty animals for a bath. Gus, finished with his phone call, motioned the riders over and introduced them as Andrea and Robert. Andrea, who had ridden Orphan, wore a big, toothy, grin. Robert looked depressed.

Gus quizzed the two riders.

"Robert, were you holding back?" Gus demanded.

"No, sir."

"Midnight's won every race this spring."

"I know."

"What happened?"

"I . . . I'm not sure."

"Trouble at the gate?"

"Not that I could tell. I thought both horses had a clean get-away."

"You gave her free rein?"

"Yes, sir. And I was laying on the stick—yelling in her ear—everything I could do to urge her on."

"But she wouldn't respond?"

"Hey, I thought she ran the hardest I've ever seen her run. What was her time?"

"I don't have Midnight's time," Gus replied.

"How about Orphan's?" Andrea asked.

"I'm not sure. I think I may have miscued the stopwatch."

"You have a readout?" Andrea asked.

Gus held up the timer, the red LED-numbers still showing 17.94 seconds.

"Wow." Andrea exclaimed.

Gus held up his other hand, a gesture of caution. "Probably a false reading."

"Since Midnight was only a length behind, that means her time would probably be eighteen point one or less?" Robert noted. "Gus, that's a very good time for 350 yards."

Gus pushed a button to clear the readout. "Listen, everyone. This is how rumors get started. Don't say anything about today's time to anyone. We've got more trials to run and only repeated time trials will tell if Orphan's really this fast."

Andrea and Robert left. I had the feeling Gus' admonition to keep the 17.94 time a secret had fallen on deaf ears. These two riders were anxious to tell their friends about beating a world record.

Gus changed the subject, "We need to start thinking about taking Orphan to Ruidoso."

"When?" Liz asked.

"I recommend early May. About a month from now."

"Does he need to be in New Mexico four months?" Liz asked.

"That would be the standard. Four months is the schedule I have planned for my best horses, the ones that are competing for the All American Futurity."

"When do we have to decide?" I asked.

"No rush. I plan to go the first weekend in May. You can bring Orphan any time after that."

We said our goodbyes and started walking back to the parking lot at the south end of the barn. As we neared our Chevy Suburban, a sleek, white Jaguar with New Mexico plates pulled up and parked. While I couldn't see the face of the driver, the large silhouette looked familiar.

Maggie and Liz climbed into our vehicle, but my curiosity got the best of me. I paused to turn back and look.

It was Edgar Payne.

CHAPTER 37

New York City

It makes no sense to me how the airline industry prices their fares. I liked it better when there was a set price and it was published in a little booklet like bus tickets. Since deregulation, the cost of an airfare varies from an unbelievable bargain to some outrageous figure that defies understanding. For example, there is no logic to the fact that, for this particular trip, a roundtrip ticket on Continental Airlines, which flies through Houston, should cost $100 less than American, which has the shorter route through Dallas.

So we played the air wars game. I bought our three tickets on Continental, flew an extra 400 miles out of the way, saved $300, and booked a room at the Plaza Hotel.

Liz had subleased her little apartment on Amsterdam Avenue to one of her opera friends and wanted to stay with her. We chose to squander our entire airfare savings—and then some—by staying at one of New York's most expensive hotels.

The Plaza, located at the corner of 59th and Sixth Avenue, just across the street from Central Park, is one of the great historic hotels in America. Maggie and I asked for an upgrade to the Plaza's concierge floor and a room overlooking the park. Pricey but luxurious—Maggie loved it.

Wednesday our family returned to the Sloan Kettering. Dr. Strong remembered us and welcomed Liz like a celebrity—a leukemia patient who had survived Graft versus Host Disease. Maggie and I spent most of the day in the twelfth-floor waiting room, but after Liz's tests, we were included in the conference at the end of the day. Dr. Strong introduced us to his colleague, Dr. Nuñez, and their two interns—the Panel of four doctors who had reviewed Liz's case and conducted her examination.

"So you're the donor?" Dr. Strong asked, shaking my hand.

I wasn't sure if the implication was good or bad. I nodded.

"Yes," Liz answered for me. "It was my dad's bone marrow that brought the GvHD cure."

Dr. Strong beamed. "Too bad we can't use you for all our BMTs." He gestured for us to take chairs at the conference table.

Maggie reached over and patted my hand.

"What's the verdict?" I asked. "Is she cured?"

The doctor quit smiling. "This is a cancer hospital. We don't use the word *cured*."

I rephrased my question. "Cancer free?"

"Yes," he replied, "cancer free . . . for now."

"It's been almost seven months since the GvHD attack," I said.

Strong opened his file folder. "Six months, three weeks, and two days."

Everyone in the room knew the next question. I decided not to ask it.

We waited.

Strong voiced it, "So the question is, will it come back?"

No one spoke.

"And the answer comes in the statistics."

He walked over to a whiteboard—a display board mounted on the wall. Using colored markers, he drew a chart while he talked.

"For the first thirty days after the attack, Liz's chances were fifty-fifty." He marked the numbers up high on the left side of his drawing.

"Medical histories of GvHD patients have shown us that, after 365 days, almost all survivors have remained cancer free for the rest of their lives." He marked a big zero on the lower right side, and then drew a diagonal line across the chart from 50 percent down to zero.

"Unfortunately, GvHD reoccurrence doesn't follow a perfectly straight line like the one I've drawn." He drew twelve vertical marks along the descending line and marked them with percentages. "If the disease acted like our statistical model, we could say Liz's chances for a return of the disease would now be at the seven-month mark, or approximately 21 percent."

He put the markers on the tray below the board and wiped his hands with a Kleenex.

"You are saying," Liz interjected, "that, as each day passes, it is statistically less likely the disease will reoccur."

Dr. Strong nodded vigorously. "Exactly. That's the good news."

"And that next September, even after having been cancer free for eleven months, the disease might still return?"

"It has happened," he replied. "There remains a small chance— we think it's statistically about 4 percent."

Liz interrupted. "Earlier, did I hear you say 'almost,' that, after one year, *almost* all GvHD patients have remained cancer free?"

The other doctor stood. "I'm fifty-six years old, and I've been here at MSKCC for twenty-nine years. I've never known a leukemia patient who survived GvHD for one year to have a reoccurrence of the disease. This doesn't mean it can't happen. It does tell us that it's so rare as to be statistically insignificant."

Dr. Strong smiled. "I guess what we're trying to say is that, in medicine, there are no guarantees."

That's okay," Liz said. "I'll take the *statistically insignificant* answer."

Everyone in the room chuckled or laughed—a welcome release from talk about the probability of death.

"Any questions?" Dr. Strong asked.

I'm sure Maggie had some, but neither she nor I raised them.

"Thank you," Liz said.

The doctors took that as a signal to stand. Maggie and I followed, and then we all shook hands.

Liz hugged Dr. Strong, after which he walked us to the elevator.

"When are you going to be singing in one of our operas?" Strong asked.

"I have an appointment tomorrow with Robert Van House to ask him that very question," Liz answered.

"Would a medical endorsement from me help?"

"It might."

He pulled out a card and gave it to her. "You could have him call me if he has any questions."

"Should he wait until next October?"

He smiled. "I could give him a stronger, less equivocal answer."

We left on that high note, and I hoped we'd never have to return.

That night we picked up Katherine and went to dinner at Daniel's, a horrendously expensive restaurant on East 76th Street. I ordered a bottle of Dom Perignon to celebrate Liz's clean bill of health.

It was a memorable, happy, upbeat evening. So much so that even the inspector general—my mother-in-law—couldn't find anything to criticize.

And I didn't say a word when she drank half the champagne.

CHAPTER 38

The Metropolitan Opera, Lincoln Center

The next day we went to hear Liz sing.

Maggie and I sat in the darkened auditorium with three other people—Robert Van House, executive director of the Met, and two of the world's most famous sopranos, Suzanne Griggs and Roberta Fancher. I put my arm around my wife and squeezed as Liz sang the opening notes of "Un bel di,"—"One Fine Day"—the most familiar melody from Puccini's *Madam Butterfly,* and one of the most beloved in all of operatic literature. It held special meaning at this audition because we all knew it as the aria Liz never got to sing two years ago on that fateful night when we learned she had leukemia.

To my untrained ear, Liz sounded better than ever.

Note after note soared out into the hall with a beautiful, effortless intensity. It carried an emotional, human message that words could never express, and I felt the adrenaline surging through me like electricity.

Maggie put her lips to my ear and whispered., "Not so tight."

Only then did I realize I was holding onto her with all my might.

ORPHAN

Maggie pulled a Kleenex from her purse and dabbed her eyes.

I withdrew my arm and gestured for one. As I wiped the tears, I looked down the row to see that Van House, Griggs, and Fancher were also wiping their eyes.

Liz finished the song.

The lights came up.

All five of us stood and clapped. And clapped. And wore out our hands. Van House yelled bravo, over and over.

Sometimes people use the expression, "Words fail me." And in my lifetime I can remember one or two times when something—a thought or a feeling—was so difficult to communicate that it could not be put into words. One such instance, a moment of supreme sadness for me, occurred twenty years ago at the funeral of my father. When pallbearers carried his coffin from the hearse to the grave, I thought of how much he had done for me and how little I had thanked him. It struck me with such intensity that I still tear up when I recall the poignancy of that moment.

Now, Liz's singing hit me with the same force—with one major difference. These were tears of joy. As I watched those around me, I sensed that they, too, were touched by two aspects of the aria: it was beautifully sung, and it came from the heart. It was an emotional performance, by someone who had survived great hardship.

We lingered on the stage a few minutes expressing our congratulations. Then Liz went to the executive director's office for a conference with Fancher and Griggs.

Maggie and I excused ourselves and went to visit the Met's store, a treasure house of opera memorabilia.

Thirty minutes later Liz joined us, and we took a cab to The Carnegie Deli—my all-time favorite delicatessen and home of New

York's most legendary corned beef sandwich.

"How'd it go?" Maggie asked the moment the waitress left with our orders.

"Wonderful," Liz said. "Van House suggested the three of us do a concert, together."

"The three sopranos?" I asked.

"A female response to The Three Tenors?" Maggie continued.

Liz took a sip of her Coke. "Plus the Texas factor. Suzanne's from Lubbock."

"We add Bushland, that famed metropolitan center of West Texas opera."

It seemed ludicrous that anyone could care about such a tiny little village in one of the least populated areas of the country.

"When?" Maggie asked.

"Mom, right now it's only an idea," Liz cautioned. "This may never happen."

"Sopranos too competitive to appear on the same stage?" I asked.

"It's pretty scary," Liz replied. "I'm not sure I want to be compared to Griggs and Fancher."

I chimed in, "Or that they'd want to be compared to a young whippersnapper like you."

"Dad."

"Seems to me they have more to lose than you."

"They're world class," she wailed. "I'm not much more than a beginner."

"Everyone has to have a 'breakout' performance. Yours just happened to be interrupted by a little illness."

"I have a request," Liz said.

Whenever I heard those words, I knew what they meant—she wanted to change the subject. I decided to do it for her, "You want to wait and see?"

"Please."

Our corned beef sandwiches came. I ate half of mine and asked for a box.

On a beautiful spring afternoon we talked about Liz's good health and the prospects for re-launching her singing career. Things couldn't be better.

Outside on the sidewalk, we made plans. I dreaded the evening, but there was no graceful way to avoid it—a trip to Brooklyn and dinner at Katherine's flat. Liz headed back to her tiny apartment. Maggie and I walked to the Plaza. We agreed to share a taxi and pick her up at seven.

That night surprised me. The festive mood of the day carried the evening, and for the second meal in two days, my mother-in-law failed to complain about anything.

What was the world coming to?

CHAPTER 39

Friday in Manhattan, Our Last Day in New York

Maggie and Liz went shopping for clothes. I hit the bookstores looking for information about horseracing. I found lots of books, but mostly about thoroughbreds. Quarter-horse racing didn't seem to interest the eastern establishment.

Friday evening we had tickets to a performance at the Met—*Das Rheingold* by Wagner. We saw posters all over Manhattan, and I was intrigued by the fact that every sign carried a special admonition in large letters, "Absolutely no one admitted after the performance has started." We arranged to meet Liz in the opera house lobby at 7:00., thirty minutes before curtain time.

"Don't be late," she said.

This was my first occasion to attend a Wagnerian Opera. The program notes gave extended information, which I read with interest. The booklet listed *Das Rheingold* as the first of four operas called the *Ring of Nibelungen,* a tetralogy using the same characters, setting, and continuing story. As I read about an opera cycle that ran for four nights, it seemed like a bit much. If my daughter

176

were to pursue a career in opera, I'd have to do some brushing up.

I was totally absorbed, reading about Wagner, when at precisely 7:30 p.m., the lights went down, we applauded the conductor, and the performance started. Four hours later—let me say that again, *four hours later*—it was over, and I made a dash for the men's room. I couldn't believe there had been no intermission. Glorious music, but more than I was expecting. And those signs about "no one admitted late" now had special meaning.

At our parting, we made arrangements for the next morning to share a cab with Liz. She wanted us to pick her up at her apartment at 6:30 a.m. in order to make our 9:30 flight to Texas. It seemed awfully early, but the drive to LaGuardia took an hour, and airline regulations demanded that passengers arrive two hours early. We did it—standard procedure for flying in the post-nine-eleven world. Then we had to stand around and wait for boarding. I didn't care. Life for our daughter was wonderful. I thought about our very good fortune.

Each passing day the ominous threat of cancer receded farther from our lives. Nothing was more important.

Liz's singing appeared poised for a future of incredible promise. I couldn't remember, ever, a performance that moved people to tears the way her Puccini aria had done. To have been there and witnessed the emotion was a blessing—a unique, once-in-a-lifetime experience. I had to pinch myself to be sure I wasn't dreaming.

Continental finally announced their boarding call for Flight 533 to Houston, ending my reverie. I felt a bounce in my step as we headed down the jet way.

We arrived home an hour late on a rainy April afternoon. While we waited at the luggage carousel, conversation returned to a topic we hadn't discussed for four days—Orphan.

"Want to go with me to check on him?" I asked.

"No," Maggie said.

"Yes," Liz answered.

We drove home in the rain.

In West Texas, any rainy day is a beautiful day, but the more I thought about it, tromping around in a muddy stable didn't have much appeal. As we carried our suitcases into the house, I discussed it with Liz.

"How about postponing our visit with Orphan?" I asked.

"Sure. Tomorrow morning?"

"Let's check the forecast."

After we settled the luggage, Liz turned on the TV Weather Channel.

"Local Weather on the 8s" predicted rain ending about midnight and a cloudless sunny day on Saturday with a high in the low 80s.

"What time tomorrow morning?" she asked.

"Let's give the mud puddles some time to dry," I suggested. "How about going right after lunch?"

She agreed and went to the piano.

I sat down at the kitchen table to sift through the mail.

Maggie picked up a notepad, a pencil, and went to the telephone answering machine.

Five minutes later she returned, her face white. "Honey, you need to come listen to this."

"What's the matter?" I asked.

She shook her head and walked away, back toward the phone in the other room. I followed.

She pushed the button and the machine gave the day, date, and time: "Wednesday, April 9, four-sixteen p.m."

I recognized the voice of our horse trainer. He sounded strained, apprehensive.

"Jim Bob, this is Gus. I'm calling to let you know we can't find Orphan. We went to his stall for the four o'clock feeding and he wasn't there. I've reported this to the Randall County Sheriff's Office. Give me a call when you get this message."

CHAPTER 40

At Home in Bushland

"When?" I asked, gripping the phone so hard my knuckles ached.

"Day before yesterday," Gus replied.

"What's happened since?"

"We contacted the county sheriff, the local police, the state authorities—all the area veterinarians and farriers."

"You're sure he's stolen, that he didn't just walk off?"

"The sheriff found tire tracks on the south side of the barn. Someone backed a horse trailer up to the door."

"In broad daylight?"

"Probably during the lunch hour on Wednesday."

"Gus, how could this happen?" It seemed incomprehensible that a horse thief could operate during the day, in full view of all the employees of a busy training stable.

Gus gave me a lecture about how horse trailers come and go, that each groom has to focus on a particular task, or on the specific stall and horse. A new trailer backs up to the door frequently. Horses come and go. It's normal, and workers are not expected to stop and ask questions.

I could see his viewpoint, and the probability that the theft happened during the lunch hour, a time when Gus went to the house for an hour's rest.

Gus changed the subject. "Jim Bob, do you have photographs of Orphan?"

"Yes, of course," I replied.

"Could you bring them here?"

I turned to Maggie. "They want snapshots of Orphan. How soon can we get them and take them to the training stable?"

"Give me thirty minutes. I'll ask Liz to help." She turned to go, and I called after her.

"I told Gus we'd drive to his place and be there with as many photos as we could find. He said he'd contact the sheriff to meet with us.

An hour later, on a dreary, rainy, late afternoon, we drove up to the familiar red barn and parked next to two Randall County Sheriff's cruisers. Inside we found a somber gathering of seven people with long faces. Standing next to Orphan's empty stall were Gus and two of his riders, Robert and Andrea, along with four men in uniform. I recognized Chief Deputy Joe Richardson, the auctioneer. He made the introductions—Sheriff Harold Lawson and two deputies from their CSI unit. I introduced Maggie and Liz.

"We brought all the pictures we had," Maggie said, handing them to Sheriff Lawson.

Lawson passed them to the CSI officers, and proceeded to give us a report of the investigation.

They had contacted all local radio stations, television stations, newspapers, magazines, horse clubs, and the American Quarter Horse Association. They had also phoned the hotlines of two national horse theft organizations.

Stolen Horse International, SHI, an independent network of horse people based in Shelby, North Carolina, would activate their volunteers through a website. SHI members, over a thousand strong, would in turn spread the word through e-mails and fliers. They promised to post information at auction yards, slaughterhouses, tack shops, holding pens, and horse shows throughout the country.

The Horse Identification Program, HIP, a theft prevention division of the Southwestern Cattle Raisers Association would mobilize their staff of thirty law enforcement officers to start working the case. They would concentrate on their contacts with local, county, state, and national law enforcement agencies all over the U.S. by sending Orphan's vital information—description, photos, and owner data.

Lawson concluded our conference by announcing that Chief Deputy Richardson would be in charge of the investigation. He urged all of us to work closely with Richardson and report any leads to him immediately.

Richardson passed out business cards.

As the group disbanded, Richardson pulled me aside. "Dr. Masterson, I'd like to visit with you and Gus for a minute." He nodded toward Gus' office.

Gus led the way. I followed. As Richardson came inside, he closed the door.

"I don't think this is the work of an organized group of horse thieves," he said. "Professional thieves typically strike between one and four a.m. If two or more saddles are taken or if several barns are hit in one night, it's usually the work of a theft ring."

"I wish they would've come during the night," Gus said. "We have spotlights with motion sensors around the barn. During the day, they're useless so we turn them off."

"Let's think in a different direction," Richardson said. "You remember that asshole who caused so much commotion at the auction?"

"Edgar Payne," I said. "How could I forget?"

"Gus tells me he was here last Monday."

"Big, tall fellow, sharp dresser, very friendly," Gus said. "He asked about training fees. Wanted to know if I had openings for two of his horses."

I nodded. "The first time I met him he was affable, easygoing, friendly—the epitome of a pleasant gentleman."

Richardson shook his head. "I don't think we're talking about the same person."

"A classic Jekyll and Hyde personality," I said. "I've seen him when he gets ticked—like at the auction. He has such a violent temper he goes berserk."

"That's the guy," Richardson said.

"He has a hair trigger, and when it goes off, he can't control himself."

"My question," continued Richardson, "and the reason I wanted to talk to you about him—do you think he's a suspect?"

"I don't think—," Gus said.

"Yes, definitely," I answered.

Richardson looked at the two of us and scratched his head.

CHAPTER 41

Monday morning, the Randall County Sheriff's Office, Amarillo

Joe Richardson handed me a cup of coffee. I could tell by the look on his face that he had bad news.

"We know your horse was taken during the lunch hour on Wednesday," Joe said.

I nodded. "Gus and two of his grooms confirm that."

"Edgar Payne has a firm alibi. On Wednesday he was attending a noon luncheon of the Albuquerque Chamber of Commerce. Fifty people can attest to his presence."

I sipped my coffee and thought for a moment. "Doesn't necessarily clear him," I said, thinking of other possibilities.

"What do you mean?"

"Payne would never do the dirty work himself. That's not his style."

"You're saying he hired others to steal the horse for him?"

"And fix races, bribe jockeys, rig the odds—all the nefarious things he's accused of."

"Your operative word being *accused*?"

"Anna Garcia's words," I said.

Joe frowned, trying to track the name. "Garcia? The woman who was murdered year before last?"

I nodded. "Payne was the leading suspect in that case, but he had an ironclad alibi."

Joe chuckled. "You don't trust Mr. Payne much, do you?"

"My blood pressure goes up every time I hear his name. We can talk about some of your other horse thief suspects."

"That's the problem. We ain't got any."

His response stunned me. I took a long draw of coffee and tried to think. "Surely you have some ideas. What about other incidents like this?"

He slouched back in his chair. "The key motivation behind almost all horse theft is quick cash. Often illegal drug use is involved. Anything that can be turned around quickly for a few hundred dollars is considered worth stealing. Thieves typically steal more than horses, so tack, trailers, even tractors are at risk. Most horses are sold within 150 miles of the theft site, often within twenty-four hours, and can be resold as many as three times in thirty-six hours." He leaned forward. "But this case doesn't fit the norm."

"How's that?" I asked.

"Gus' barn has almost a hundred horses. Why take only one?"

"Good question."

"Dozens of expensive saddles and bridles—none were touched."

I nodded.

"We've checked all of the livestock auctions within 150 miles—nothing."

"So what exactly are you saying?"

"It looks like the thieves had a single objective. They came to steal *your* horse. If that's the case, they know they have a $100,000 animal and will treat him accordingly. They're not taking him to the county sale barn to auction him off for $500 as a pet for some rancher's kid."

"You telling me they'll treat him like a $100,000 racehorse?"

"Wouldn't you?"

"No."

Joe looked at me as if I had Alzheimer's.

"I've been doing some homework. The guys at AQHA tell me expensive racehorses are all about bloodlines, about the identity of the sire and the dam—it goes back for generations. With DNA technology, thieves can't race him, breed him, or even sell him without papers."

"You think they'll sell him for horse meat?" Joe asked.

"No, of course not," I answered.

"Then what?"

"The minor leagues. Races where officials don't make thorough checks about bloodlines. Or perhaps they'll try to race him in a different country."

"Different country?"

"Mexico, or some place in South America." As the words left my mouth, I had a sinking feeling. If the thieves took Orphan to South America, we'd never see him again.

The phone rang. Joe turned to take the call.

I left the sheriff's office with a feeling of hopelessness. The rest of the day dragged as I moped around, trying to muster up enough energy to work on cattle. Finally, I called Paul Edwards.

"Got time for a cup of coffee?"

"Sure," he replied. "I've been hoping to talk with you about Orphan."

"Starbuck's on Georgia Street?"

"Meet you in fifteen minutes."

I called Fred, my associate, and Ida Mae, my secretary, into the office and asked them to take over. They understood.

I drove to Starbuck's and found Paul sitting at a small table by the front window with two cups of coffee.

"Thanks for the caffeine," I said, sliding in across from him.

"Hope you like hazelnut cream," he replied.

"Right now, I'd drink anything."

"That bad?"

"I never dreamed it would be so easy to steal a horse, nor so difficult to trace a horse thief."

"Welcome to the club." Paul tore open a second pink packet of sweetener, dumped it into the paper cup, and stirred it with his plastic spoon.

"You have any experience with animal theft?" I asked.

"More than I want. My CPA tells me 45,000 horses a year are stolen in the United States and Canada."

"Makes you sick to even think about it."

"It's worse for cattle." He continued to move his spoon around in his coffee cup. "Twice that many were taken last year."

"Why doesn't law enforcement do something?"

"I think they're trying, but to be effective, the public must get involved. People like you and me have got to pitch in."

"Hell, I'm motivated. What can I do?"

"Take off from your job. Work on it fulltime. Contact friends like me. Ask for help. Go after the bad guys like you mean business."

I thought about his suggestions.

"I've sent an e-mail to the Texas Cattle Feeders Association," he continued. "We've asked all our members to contribute to an 'Orphan Reward' fund. So far we've received $24,500. We'd like you to post the reward."

"Paul, I wish you hadn't done that. This is my problem."

"Hey. These guys want to help you. Let . . . them . . . do it."

CHAPTER 42

At Home, Bushland

Paul was right, again. Money talks. The big reward offered by TCFA generated an unbelievable response.

I set up an office at home. I followed his advice about working fulltime on horse theft. Fred and Ida Mae took over the veterinary clinic. Maggie and Liz pitched in, and we organized a three-person team to answer calls, receive faxes, respond to e-mails, and mount a nationwide media blitz. Almost overnight, we went from no suspects to hundreds.

We converted the dining room into something that looked like a branch post office. At the center of this whirlwind of activity was a flyer Liz designed. Printed on letter-size paper, it featured full-color photographs of Orphan, including close-ups of his identifying markings. At first we printed a thousand copies. The next day we printed another five thousand. When those were gone, we called the printer and asked for twenty-five thousand more.

Mailing labels came from everywhere—the association of horse traders, a feed company's list of retail stores, sale barns, horse clubs, the AQHA Journal's listing of subscribers, law enforcement agencies, newspapers, magazines, broadcast media. Every day we picked up another set of addresses. When volunteers asked what they could do to help, we made a place for them at the dining room table, gave them a stack of flyers, a set of mailing labels, and put them to work.

Maggie took charge of the house. Liz went out to horse sales where she circulated among the buyers, posting flyers, and putting them on windshields.

Joe Richardson became a daily presence in my life. He set up a standing appointment for me at the sheriff's office. Every morning at nine o'clock I drove to the corner of Georgia Street and Hollywood Road, and we exchanged information, reviewed leads, plotted strategy. Joe was terrific. And he brought clout to our search—the rhetorical, as well as official—long arm of the law.

Each day Joe and I sorted through all our leads. On Saturday morning, an e-mail from a guy named George Woods looked promising. George had found two horses—both believed to be stolen—one of which matched the description of Orphan. Joe suggested we drive to see George in Lexington, Kentucky, so we jumped into my Chevy Suburban and started east on I-40 for the eighteen-hour trip. We never made it to Lexington. While we were in route Maggie called about a Sunday afternoon rodeo in Nashville.

"This man is head of the Davidson County Rodeo," she said. "He wants to claim the reward."

"What did he say?"

"He's found a guy trying to sell a horse he thinks is Orphan. The guy's pickup and his horse trailer have Texas plates."

Joe called the Davidson County Sheriff's Office. They arranged to have two deputies meet us at the rodeo.

We made our way to the rodeo grounds, met the deputies, and examined the horse. It wasn't Orphan. We spent the afternoon posting flyers and looking at every horse on the premises.

By the end of the day, we were exhausted. We checked into a Holiday Inn and slept for twelve hours.

The next morning we grabbed some breakfast and reviewed our strategy.

"Too many leads," I said.

"I agree," Joe replied, "but you have to admit, when we arrived yesterday afternoon, we both thought this rodeo looked promising."

"Uh huh, but why would a thief bring a $100,000 racehorse to a regional rodeo, a thousand miles away, where they're likely to check his bloodline?"

Joe agreed. "Yeah, now that we've seen the event—"

"Personally, I don't think this was a good place to sell him?"

Joe sipped his coffee. "The distance was good. The site wasn't."

"What would be a good site?" I asked.

"Some place where they pay big bucks for racehorses."

"Ruidoso, New Mexico."

Joe shook his head. "Too close. I'll bet every horse trader in New Mexico knows Orphan's been stolen."

I agreed. "Yeah, they'd be looking for him."

"Name the most likely places, other than Texas, New Mexico, and Oklahoma, where expensive racehorses are traded and sold."

"California and Kentucky?"

"How many calls about the reward from those two states?"

I phoned Maggie and asked the same question. She gave me four names. I wrote them down and read the list to Joe.

"Santa Anita and San Diego, California. Louisville and

Lexington, Kentucky."

"What was the name of that guy in Lexington?" Joe asked.

I pulled his email from my briefcase. George Woods. Let's get on the road."

CHAPTER 43

Monday afternoon, Churchill Downs, Louisville, Kentucky

My first visit to thoroughbred country exceeded all expectations. From Louisville to Lexington, a distance of seventy-five miles, Joe and I found dozens of horse farms. Beautiful green pastures with endless white rail fences and large stables, contained hundreds of horses grazing in the fields. Billboards everywhere advertised Churchill Downs and the date for the biggest event of the year—The Kentucky Derby.

I called Woods, and found he worked as a groom at the Keeneland Horse Auction near Lexington. He was large, black, and greeted us with a pronounced Kentucky drawl. We learned immediately that he had an extensive knowledge of thoroughbred racing.

"We're anxious to hear what you've found," I said.

"And I'm interested in your reward," he replied.

"What can you tell us?"

"White Dodge pickup, pulling a big, white horse trailer complete with living quarters. New Mexico plates. Driver looked Hispanic. The fact that he was trying to sell his horse out of his trailer caught my eye."

"Why is that suspicious?" I asked.

"This is prime time for horse trading," George replied. "The biggest auction of the year for two-year-olds is scheduled just before Derby Week."

"So?"

"So, everyone I know lists their horses in the Keeneland sale booklet," he said. "Owners usually want as much publicity as they can get. This guy's just the opposite. He didn't include his horse in the auction, and he seemed to be going out of his way to avoid publicity."

"Where is he now?" Joe asked.

"Driving around. Probably over by the stables, trying to make a private sale."

I looked at Joe. "How do you want to do this?"

"Let's go looking." He turned to George. "We'd like you to go with us."

"Give me five minutes." He made arrangements called to his co-workers to cover for him, exchanged his boots for shoes, and climbed into the back seat of the Suburban.

We followed his directions to the racetrack, located nearby. George knew the security guards on a first-name basis and used his credentials to get us into the grounds.

The stable area was huge. I guessed it to be a quarter-mile square—probably 160 acres, maybe more. George knew all the streets, lanes, and cul-de-sacs. He also knew many of the trainers, the grooms, and the riders. We stopped occasionally and waited while he asked his friends if they had seen a white pickup pulling a white horse trailer with New Mexico plates.

Almost everyone had seen the guy "yesterday."

A few had seen him driving around "this morning."

No one had seen him this afternoon.

After about two hours we arrived back at the gate.

"Could you pull over?" George asked. "Let's talk."

I stopped.

"Obviously, he's not here this afternoon," he said.

Joe was skeptical. "Maybe we missed him. I think we should make another pass."

"We have time," I added.

George looked at his watch. "It's not good to be nosing around after dark. People get jumpy about protecting their horses at night."

"How much time do we have before the sun goes down?" I asked.

"An hour. Maybe a little more."

We started the second round, stopping at other stables. Each time Joe got out and went with George. Time after time, stop after stop, people gave us the same answer. Yes, they'd seen the pickup and trailer, but not "this afternoon." After dozens of stops, and just as the sun dropped below the western horizon, George found a stable with some news.

Joe motioned for me to join them in a small horse barn at the end of a cul-de-sac.

I turned off the Suburban's engine, grabbed my keys, and hurried into the building to find George questioning a young, black groom.

"White Dodge pulling a white trailer, both with New Mexico plates? You sure?" George asked.

"Yeah, a Mexican driver," the groom answered. "He was showing his horse to another driver with a pickup and trailer."

"Can you describe the other rig?"

"Sure."

We waited while he stood there, closed mouthed.

"How much is it worth to you?" the groom finally asked.

Joe pulled out a $100 bill and tore it in two. He handed half to the groom. "Depends on how much you can tell us."

"The other pickup was a white Ford," the groom said. "She was pulling a small maroon trailer."

"She?" Joe asked.

"Yeah."

"I think I know the rig," George said. "Belongs to a woman veterinarian from Florida."

The groom nodded. "That's the one."

"What else can you tell us?" George asked.

"The two of 'em spent quite a while looking over the Mexican's horse," he answered. "He walked him around while she watched."

"Describe the horse," I said.

"Good-looking chestnut. I didn't see it up close."

"White blaze? Four white socks? Diamond-WT brand on the rump?"

The groom shook his head. "Like I say, I didn't see him up close."

"Anything else?" Joe asked.

"I haven't told you the most important thing." The groom held up his half of the bill. "I was waiting for the rest of this."

Joe gave him the other half. "Better be good."

The young man grinned for a moment, adding to the suspense. "She took the horse and loaded it into her trailer."

ORPHAN

"Then what happened?"

"He drove off one way. She went the other."

CHAPTER 44

Tuesday, Keeneland Auction, Lexington, Kentucky

We spent the next day looking for the two rigs—especially for the one with the small maroon trailer. White pickups and white horse trailers were everywhere, but we had something else to look for: New Mexico plates on one, and probably—we were guessing—Florida plates on the other.

The effort proved to be an exercise in frustration. We didn't find either. It reminded me of the proverbial black hole—two horse trailers swallowed up without a trace.

While I drove, Joe spent hours on his phone contacting state police in Tennessee, Georgia, and Florida—asking them to watch the interstate highways for the Ford and the small maroon trailer. He also called authorities in Tennessee, Arkansas, Oklahoma, Texas, and New Mexico to be on the lookout for the other rig.

When the day finally ended, we had nothing.

That night, after I called home, I tossed and turned, slept fitfully, and awoke the next morning tired and depressed. Joe met me in the coffee shop for breakfast.

"You don't look so hot," he said.

I tried a smile that failed. "Neither do you."

"Obviously, they're gone."

I nodded.

"I'm ready to drive back to Amarillo. How about you?"

"Sure," I replied.

We finished breakfast, packed, and headed West—taking turns at the wheel. Twenty hours later, I dropped him off at the Randall County Sheriff's Office and continued on to Bushland. The sun was just peeking over the eastern horizon as I turned off I-40 and drove the last two miles north to our ranch. When I pulled into our driveway, Maggie heard me and came running out the kitchen door. She held out her arms and gave me a crushing bear hug. With our arms wrapped around each other, she whispered, "I've missed you."

"Me, too." I said, holding her close.

After several minutes, I relaxed, and as Maggie dropped her arms I saw tears in her eyes.

"Want some breakfast?" she asked as she wiped her face with the back of her hand.

"After a shower," I replied, giving her shoulders another squeeze.

The cascading water felt wonderful, and I lingered until the hot ran out. Then I struggled into pajamas, robe, and slippers, so tired I could have fallen asleep on my feet, but the aroma of Maggie's hot biscuits, ham, and eggs revived me.

"Want to tell me about the trip," she asked. "Or do you want to just eat first?"

"Nothing to tell," I mumbled, my mouth full of food. "We struck out."

"What about the woman vet with the maroon horse trailer?"

Clearly, Maggie's question about "eating first" had been a rhetorical one. She wanted to talk. I wanted to eat. She waited a moment, then continued a one-sided conversation.

"We're getting dozens of leads." She pushed a list across the table.

With my mouth full, I scanned the information.

"We've sent out almost 50,000 flyers," Maggie said. "And we've exhausted all of the mailing labels." She rattled on, telling me about our volunteers and the data they had assembled. I finished the ham and eggs, buttered the last biscuit, and tried to concentrate on the list of suspects, but my brain clouded over and refused to accept new information.

"You awake?" she asked. "You look like a zombie."

I put the list down. "How about we tackle this after I've slept for a few hours?"

She put her arm around me as we tottered down the hall to our bedroom. I plopped down on the bed. She pulled the covers over me. Ten seconds later I was gone.

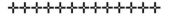

The next thing I knew, Maggie was gently shaking my shoulder. "Joe Richardson is on the phone," she said. "He says it's important."

I blinked, tried to think. "What time is it?"

"Four o'clock in the afternoon. You've slept almost ten hours."

"Hello," I squeaked.

"You okay?" Joe asked, his words bright, upbeat.

"How can you be so damn cheerful?"

"We may have some good news."

"Call me tomorrow when I'm awake."

"I'm flying to Miami in the morning. Wanna go?"

"Miami?"

"The Dade County Sheriff called. He's found a female veterinarian with a maroon horse trailer."

I sat up, wide-awake.

Joe continued, "She has six horses booked on a plane flying to Mexico City on Thursday."

"What's today?"

"Tuesday."

"So she's shipping them out day after tomorrow?"

"You're awake? You can read the calendar?"

I ignored his sarcasm. "Has anybody seen these horses?"

"Yes. One of them is a chestnut with a white blaze who used to have four white socks."

"What do you mean, *used to*?"

"She colored them."

I gripped the phone. "What flight are you booked on?"

"*We*," he said. "We're booked on American Airlines, leaving at 5:45 a.m. The Sheriff's Sale is paying for your ticket."

CHAPTER 45

Miami International Airport

Two Miami-Dade policemen met us at the curb in front of the
terminal driving green-and-gold-striped cruisers. They introduced
themselves as Dennis and Manuel. Dennis was huge—at least 300
pounds. Manuel was my height, about five-seven, Hispanic, and
looked like he lifted weights—a lot. He spoke with an accent. Joe
rode with the big deputy. Manuel and I followed in the second car.

"One of these horses is yours?" he asked."

"Yes," I replied, describing Orphan's identifying marks.

"He's expensive racehorse?"

"I paid a hundred thousand dollars for him."

"Mi Dios. That much for a horse?"

"He's very fast."

"We get him for you."

"I hope."

With flashing red and blue lights, we drove to the cargo area of
Miami International Airport. Two other Miami-Dade police cars
were parked out on the tarmac near the loading ramp for an old

Boeing 707. As we drove up, I could see horses being taken onto the plane.

I watched from the car as Joe conferred with the police and customs officials. While they talked, a cattle truck pulled up to the ramp of another plane and began unloading. The customs officials went over to check a herd of Black Angus.

Joe stood beside me.

"They have papers on six horses from the Heidi Crighton Veterinary Services in West Palm Beach," Joe reported.

"Are they on the plane?"

"Not yet, but it's scheduled to depart in two hours."

"What's our plan?"

"We're going to sit and wait for Crighton and her horse trailer."

I thought about having the two law enforcement vehicles by the loading ramp. "Aren't you afraid we'll scare them off?"

"We'll move over by those hangars. We're part of the scenery."

The deputies walked away and Joe and I watched The Port Authority officials process the cattle.

I looked at my watch—three o'clock.

The next hour dragged on. Two additional horse trailers brought horses and loaded them on the plane. Neither was from Crighton Veterinary Services. After a few minutes, Manuel returned and walked me to the plane. I went through, looking for—Orphan. He wasn't there. We disembarked and the plane took off for Mexico City.

Manuel went for pizza.

"There's another plane to Mexico City leaving at midnight," Dennis said. "Could be Crighton rebooked her horses to the later flight."

We decided to wait.

Darkness fell.

About nine o'clock the ground crew set up a loading ramp. Trucks came to unload horses. An hour later the pilots arrived and started making flight preparations. Again, we were taken on board to check the horses. No luck.

At 11:45 customs cleared the flight. The ground crew withdrew the loading ramp. Then, at almost exactly midnight, the engines started and the plane taxied off toward the runway.

"What about Crighton's horses?" I asked.

"They're not going to Mexico on that plane," Dennis replied.

"What happened?" Joe asked.

"Damned if I know."

"Manuel, do you have the address of the vet's clinic in West Palm Beach?" I asked.

"We can get it."

Dennis and Joe got into one of the cruisers—Manuel and I into the other. As we drove north to the address, I wondered why someone hadn't gone to the clinic in the first place. I thought about quizzing Manuel about it, but he brought it up before I could comment.

"We should've set up the arrest earlier, but headquarters wanted us to wait on you."

"Why?" I asked.

"They thought we needed you to identify your horse."

"When did you last have surveillance of my horse?"

"This morning," he replied. "We had two officers staked out across the street from the clinic. They reported that Crighton loaded the horses into two trailers at one o'clock."

"Just about the time we landed?"

"Yeah, that's why we went straight to the cargo loading area."

"Did anyone follow the horses?"

He shook his head. "They didn't want to alert the suspects."

The car in front slowed and turned off its flashing lights. Manuel did the same.

We rode in silence into the Crighton Veterinary Services parking lot. All the buildings were dark. The four of us got out and walked the grounds, peering in windows, inspecting the pens.

No people.

No animals.

The place was deserted.

CHAPTER 46

Miami, Florida

I confess. I used to think of law enforcement as a cushy job—good salary, lots of perks, and little or no hard work.

No more.

After striking out at the Crighton Veterinary Services, the Miami guys dropped us off at a Motel 6 at three a.m. I fell into bed and recounted the hours—up at four, drove to the Amarillo airport, catch a 5:45 flight, land in Miami, chase the bad guys—a twenty-three-hour day. And that wasn't the worst part . . . the alarm went off at six a.m.

By 6:30 Joe and I met the officers at a waffle place next door to the motel. Manny trumped my hard-luck story when he told us about going after a search warrant. Apparently, he'd had no sleep.

I scaled back my martyr's rhetoric, ate a quick breakfast, and joined the others for our trip back to the vet clinic. Like the day before, I rode with Manuel.

He looked terrible.

"Want me to drive?"

He blinked, wiping his eyes. "State law. Only uniformed per-sonnel are allowed to operate law enforcement vehicles."

I could see my job—keep Manuel awake. I did my best to man-ufacture conversation. Twenty minutes later, and with a sense of relief, we pulled into the parking lot at Crighton Veterinary Clinic.

As a DVM I've been around vet facilities all my adult life. I know what to expect—this wasn't it. In fact, I would say it was the poorest excuse for an animal clinic I'd ever seen. The building was filthy. Obviously Heidi Crighton did not have an active veterinary practice. I guessed she only used the clinic as a site to keep stolen animals—like my horse.

We did find one important bit of evidence—a hair coloring kit.

During our morning search, a neighbor stopped to visit. He told us he came to the place two days ago to complain to Dr. Crighton about the smell. She promised she would work on it because she wanted to sell the clinic and move back to Illinois. At the time he thought he recognized one of the horses, a palomino that had been reported missing from a nearby polo match.

In every other way, our morning search revealed nothing. No clues to Crighton's whereabouts, to her plans, or what had happened to the horses.

Another dead end.

"How often do ships dock in Miami and pick up horses going to Mexico or to South America?" I asked.

"It's against the law to send horses by ship," Dennis replied.

"Really?"

"Years ago, horses were so mistreated that a law was passed requiring them to be shipped by air."

"I didn't know that."

"Been on the books a long time," he said. "Longer than I've been in law enforcement."

We decided to break for lunch at a nearby burger place.

"Back to Miami International?" I asked.

"It's our best lead," Manuel replied.

"Waiting around, checking every cargo plane ain't my favorite assignment," Dennis said.

"Then I'll do it," I said. "Get me the authority, the clearance, and I'll baby-sit the airport."

"We need to check with the highway patrol. Alert them to be on the lookout for stolen horses."

"It wouldn't hurt to post a stakeout at the vet clinic," Dennis added.

"Do you have the manpower to do this?" Joe asked.

"For a limited time," Dennis said.

"How long?"

"Probably a week or so, depending on what else comes along. If we have a bank robbery or some big case, we'll have to let this go."

"Of course," Joe said.

We dispersed. The Miami guys dropped us at Hertz to rent two cars. Joe took his and went to the Miami-Dade Headquarters. I drove to the airport, and my luck changed. The only plane that could take horses was departing at four p.m. I checked it out, then went back to the motel and crawled into bed.

The next few days settled into a boring sameness. Joe and I met for breakfast. He'd drive off to the police headquarters, and I'd go to the airport. Most days we'd meet for dinner and compare notes. The evening meals were the most depressing part of the day because the news was always bad. Heidi Crighton and her horse trailers had fallen off the radar.

On May first, our seventh day in Miami, Joe broke the bad news.

"Jim Bob, I'm going to have to go back to work in Randall County."

"I understand," I said, but I couldn't hide my disappointment.

"What're your plans?"

"I guess I'll keep the watch at Miami International."

He nodded. "That's our best lead."

The next morning Joe turned in his rental car and flew back to Amarillo. Manuel and Dennis were pulled off the case and dispatched to a gang fight in Dade County. Our horse-thief detail became a task force of one. Me.

A week went by.

Another week came and went, memorable only for bad food and bad news.

One of the things that kept me going was a nightly phone call to Maggie and Liz. As the fourth week started, Maggie asked the inevitable question, "When are you coming home?"

"Soon," I said, knowing my answer sounded evasive.

"You can't stay in Miami forever."

I clenched my teeth at the thought of failure.

"How about tomorrow?" she asked. "I miss you."

Maggie was right. "Okay, I'll make one last check, and then catch an afternoon plane."

"Call me when you change planes in Dallas."

"I will."

The next morning I checked out of the motel and drove to the cargo area of Miami International Airport. I stopped at the security gate to tell the guys this would be my last time. They said their goodbyes, wished me well, and raised the gate, but just as I started to drive into the restricted area, the short "whirr" of a police siren stopped me.

Manuel and Dennis drove up—lights flashing on their cruiser.

Chapter 47

Miami International Airport

"We think we've found the horses," Manuel called from the open window.

"Where?" I asked, fresh adrenaline beginning to pump.

"Key Largo."

"The Keys?"

"South, about sixty miles—in Monroe County."

"South?" I couldn't believe it. For the past month we'd been searching all the highways to the north.

"Monroe County deputies are waiting for us. We need you to identify your horse."

"Of course. Lead the way."

They drove fast down Interstate-826 and then on the Florida Turnpike south. I struggled to hang close behind, our speeds reaching twenty miles per hour or more *over* the speed limit. Our fast pace ended at Homestead, a small town at the southernmost tip of the Florida mainland. At that point the only road south became a narrow, two-lane blacktop—U.S. 1, the infamous overseas highway.

No passing. Traffic slowed to a crawl. Thank God we didn't have to go all the way to Key West.

Fifteen miles later we came to the island of Key Largo. I could see Manny holding a microphone to his lips and guessed he was getting directions. I noticed a grocery store, honked and pointed. We pulled off the highway, and I got out of my car to confer.

"How much farther?" I asked.

"Less than five miles, I think," Dennis replied.

"I'll only be a minute." I ran into the grocery and purchased a couple of apples.

We continued south on U.S. 1 for another couple of miles before Dennis turned off the highway toward the Atlantic Ocean. I followed the Miami-Dade cruiser on a single-lane, dirt road close to the shoreline. We bounced along a rough trail at less than ten miles per hour, sometimes only a few feet from the water. Minutes later we came to a green-and-white-striped Monroe County Sheriff's car parked by an old barn. I got out and walked over with the officers. We exchanged handshakes and introductions with two uniformed Monroe deputies. They led the way through the barn and out the back door into a small pasture. The poor quality of the grass and the small size of the fenced area would not, in my opinion, be enough to sustain a horse for very long.

The five of us stopped. I counted six horses, all of which looked so malnourished their ribs showed. The herd cowered and moved away from us to the far corner of the small paddock. One of them, a chestnut, reminded me of Orphan, but the familiar markings I was hoping to find—a white blaze and white socks—weren't there.

All the law enforcement guys remained in place for a moment, watching the thin, scruffy-looking horses mill about. I walked ahead another ten yards to a point almost halfway between the humans and the horses.

The chestnut whinnied and moved out from the other horses, toward me.

I stood perfectly still.

The horse came up close and nuzzled me.

I gave him an apple. He ate it in a way I had never seen before. At first I thought, *this isn't Orphan. He'd never gobble down an apple like that,* but then I realized, I'd never been around him when he was starving.

He whinnied. He snorted. He nuzzled me.

I gave him the second of my two apples. He ate it hungrily.

I turned and walked back the short distance to the deputies. The horse followed me, his nose touching my shoulder.

The deputies were all smiles. It was obvious to everyone—we had found Orphan.

CHAPTER 48

Key Largo, Florida

The deputies called a veterinarian.

Two hours later David Bechtel, DVM, pulled up to the barn with a big rig—large enough to load all six horses. He and I spent an hour examining the animals.

Dave impressed me with his knowledge of horses. Apparently he had a big practice around Hialeah Racetrack. I especially liked his ideas about feeding malnourished horses back to good health. His nutritional approach was to go slow, offer top-grade alfalfa hay, not much grain at first, combined with a complex regimen of vitamins and minerals, and his thoughts about exercise matched mine—start easy.

Together we loaded the six starving animals into his horse trailer. I followed him back to his vet clinic near Hialeah.

On the way I used my cellphone to call home. Maggie was thrilled to receive the good news. Liz was ecstatic. I spent almost the entire hour-and-a-half drive on the phone, laughing, each of us talking over the other in our excitement, sharing all the details.

ORPHAN

The next few days passed quickly. Dave Bechtel suggested it would be better to fly Orphan back to Amarillo than to haul him 2,000 miles in a horse trailer. Dave helped me find a pilot with an old Douglas DC-3 that would transport us for a bargain $5,000. We scheduled the trip for May 30—one week from the day I'd found Orphan.

Dave recommended we give Orphan a tranquilizer, a horse-sized dose of Valium. He also suggested we fly at night, thinking Orphan would probably sleep for most of the trip.

The next morning, when we landed at Amarillo's Rick Husband International Airport, the sun was coming up on a beautiful spring day. Liz and Orphan had a wonderful reunion. Her eyes sparkled with tears as she loaded him into our horse trailer.

At the end of the thirty-minute drive home, I backed up to the loading ramp, just as I had that first time two and a half years ago, when Orphan was only two weeks old. As he took his first steps into the familiar pen, we experienced an exhilarating moment, an emotional time impossible to explain to others. All our hopes came together, all our work, all our prayers, all the times we had dreamed of and what it would be like and feel like.

Orphan knew it, too.

We watched as he pranced around the pen, as he tossed and turned his head in that old unique way. We watched the movement of his body as he circled the familiar space, the way he held his head and tail—all were the same. We watched him turn his body sideways when he stopped, something Orphan always did.

Liz crawled over the fence into the pen, whistled, and Orphan jerked his head up to face her. His movements intensified. His head and tail held high was a beautiful sight—one I had thought I might never see again. Liz held out an apple slice, and he took it. Then he did something I've never seen a horse do. He held his nose over her shoulder, the equine equivalent of a hug, for a long moment.

Liz began to rub his neck, gushing over him with soft, nonsensical words. With her other hand, she reached behind her back with another slice of apple, but Orphan didn't take it. He seemed to be more interested in her touch than in food.

She waited a few moments, and then turned around. Again she held out the apple slices and Orphan gobbled them up.

Maggie went into the pen. She just had to touch him—to rub his neck, hold him tight, kiss his nose.

After a few more minutes we turned him out into the pasture with the Black Angus, to let him run free in the rich, green, buffalo grass. Orphan loved it.

While he was running, Liz and I talked about nutrition. I gave her the Miami feed formula, the Hialeah list, and she went into the barn to measure out his rations.

"How about some breakfast?" Maggie asked.

"You bet." I looked at my watch to see that it was almost noon. I was starving.

After a quick bite I shaved, showered, and fell into bed.

Six hours later, Maggie woke me.

"Paul Edwards and Joe Richardson are here," she said.

I dressed and went out to find Joe and Paul were sitting on the fence with Liz. Orphan was munching alfalfa hay over by the door to the barn.

"He looks so thin you could use his hips for a hat rack," Paul said.

"Yeah, he's lost about two hundred pounds," I replied.

"Other than that, how's his condition?" Joe asked.

"He's fine."

"Can he race?"

"I think so," I replied. "The Miami vet thought he could be ready in about a month. I've called Gus Gonzalez. He's driving back from Ruidoso next week to look at him."

On that beautiful, late-spring evening, just a few days short of two-and-a-half years since I'd found him at the side of the highway, we were sitting on our fence, watching Orphan contentedly eating hay.

It amazed me how much this animal had changed our lives.

CHAPTER 49

Wednesday, June 4, at Home in Bushland

As expected, Gus Gonzalez drove from Ruidoso to the Amarillo area—a distance of almost three hundred miles—just to see Orphan. Liz and I walked him out to our barn.

"God, he looks skinny," Gus said.

"You should have seen him when we first found him. He went without much food for almost thirty days."

Gus climbed over the fence and picked up Orphan's hooves one at a time. Then he rubbed his coat, patted him, all the time speaking to him in soothing tones. I marveled at how Orphan responded to this trainer.

"You say you had a horse vet in Miami examine him?"

I nodded and told him about David Bechtel's qualifications. "We vaccinated and wormed him. Had a farrier trim his hooves."

Gus nodded approval.

"At first he was lethargic, but he's been on this diet for almost two weeks and he seems nearly as perky now as before he was stolen." I handed Gus a copy of what we were feeding Orphan.

Gus scanned the list and nodded. "I like your vitamins and minerals. Looks like a well-balanced diet. What about exercise?"

"None at first, but we've increased it day by day. When we started, we'd lead him from another horse. For the past four days, Liz has ridden him out for a daily gallop. He loves to run."

Gus turned to Liz. "I'd like to see you exercise him."

Liz beamed. "Sure." She went into the barn to saddle Orphan.

Gus and I walked out a couple of hundred yards into the pasture to watch. Minutes later Liz galloped the horse to the far side and back, a half-mile each way. Then she dismounted and walked him back into the barn. Gus and I talked while she hosed him off.

"Jim Bob, I'm amazed," Gus said.

"Looks good, doesn't he?"

"Far better than I expected."

"Obviously, we have the Miami vet to thank for most of this."

"Excellent advice."

"So, what do you think?"

Gus watched Orphan's bath for a few moments. Liz finished and led the horse to his stall for his afternoon feeding.

"I came here afraid it might be too late to try for the All American this year," Gus said. "Midnight Dash and all my other contenders have been training at Ruidoso for almost a month."

"So what are you saying? Do you think you can get Orphan into shape in time?"

"We need to get Liz in on this. She'll have to do some of the most important work to get him ready."

I joined Liz at Orphan's stall. "Come back outside when you're finished."

Gus gave us a rundown of things that would have to be done to get Orphan ready to compete for a place in Ruidoso's big race.

"Liz, you'll have to help," Gus told her, watching her reaction.

She smiled, flattered by Gus' attention. "I'll do whatever you ask."

"We need to move him over to my place. Can you spend twelve hours a day over there for the next week or so?"

She didn't hesitate—even for a moment. "Sure."

"Good, let's move him tomorrow. Here's what I want you do." He wrote out a list and handed it to Liz.

I stood by her and read it with interest. Much of it was the same or an expanded version of what she was already doing. The biggest difference was that he added *breeze from the gate* to Orphan's daily routine.

"From the gate?" she asked. "I've never done that."

"We'll practice it tomorrow," he said. "I'll help you."

Early the next morning, we loaded Orphan into our trailer and took him to the familiar big red barn, now featuring a security gate. A direct result of the theft.

We waited for Gus to meet us with his key. After we had Orphan situated in his same old stall—the same one from which he'd been stolen almost two months earlier—Gus led us out to the practice field. Three of his grooms were there, two mounted on horses, waiting for the starting procedures. We watched while Gus lectured.

The third groom loaded each of the horses into a gate, and prepared the starting mechanism. When he pushed the button, a loud bell started ringing, doors flew open, and the horses tore off down the track. A quarter-mile away, we could see a white flag mounted on a fencepost. The horses raced past the flag, then eased up—their riders letting them slow to a walk before they started back.

Gus introduced us to the starter, "This is Gerald McCastland. We call him Mac. During June, July, and August, while I'm in Ruidoso, Mac is in charge of the stable."

We all shook hands, then listened while Gus told Liz what he wanted her to do.

"Let me say it again. I want you to *breeze* Orphan, a short training race like the one you just saw. Your goal is to teach him how to get out of the gate quickly and safely, and to routine the feeling of competition with another horse in a short race."

Liz looked a little wary, but didn't say anything.

"I'd like you to breeze Orphan now."

"Now?" Liz asked, startled.

"Orphan's done it before. Your job is to build the routine."

Liz shrugged and gave us a half-smile. "Okay."

She left to go saddle Orphan. I stayed to hear Gus' instructions.

"The reason I want Liz to ride him is that my two best riders, Andrea and Robert, are in Ruidoso. They're doing this very same training with Midnight Dash and a couple of other horses we think have a chance to enter the All American."

"What about these two riders, the ones we just saw?" I asked.

"They're new, inexperienced."

"So is Liz."

"Yes, but she has an advantage—"

"Orphan knows her and trusts her?"

"Exactly."

A few minutes later a groom appeared riding a beautiful gray horse. Next came a chestnut. Even from a distance I could tell it was Orphan, but I didn't recognize the rider until they came close to the gate. Liz looked different in riding costume and goggles. She gave me a nervous smile.

"Catch me if I fall off," she said. I knew she meant it as a joke but the quiver in her voice gave her away. She was scared.

Mac loaded the gray horse in the gate.

Gus loaded Orphan.

"Ready?" Mac asked.

"Yep," the groom on the gray called.

"Okay," came a weak reply from Liz.

Mac pushed the button, the bell rang, and the two horses sprang from the gate. We watched the race from the back, through a cloud of dust. I thought it would be impossible, or at least difficult, to tell who won.

It wasn't.

Orphan was so far in the lead, it made the call easy.

CHAPTER 50

Masterson and Associates Veterinary Clinic

I worked at my clinic every day after returning from Florida. Fred and Ida Mae had served yeomen's duty in maintaining our business and were glad to see me. Most of our income came from contracts with large feed yards where I was on call to respond to their needs.

On my first day back, the three of us held a conference to discuss plans for the summer. Ida Mae reported that we had not lost a single account while I was gone. I had written bonus checks to each and thanked them for the good work they'd done.

"We're thinking of taking our horse to Ruidoso with the hope of entering him in the All American Futurity," I said.

"How much will you have to be gone?" Ida Mae asked.

"Weekends in June and July. Probably the entire month of August," I answered.

"Fine," Fred said. "We can handle the clinic."

"You expect to be back full time after Labor Day?" Ida Mae asked.

"Absolutely."

She didn't say it, but I could sense an undercurrent. Ida Mae wanted me here, working to build the business, whereas, Fred saw my absence as an opportunity for himself. When I was here, everyone regarded him as an assistant. When I was gone, he became the star of the show, *the* veterinarian our customers looked to for medical services. Over the first three days back, I complimented them again and again, communicate my appreciation for their good work.

On Wednesday, after we closed the clinic, I drove to the Gonzalez Training Stables to check on Liz and Orphan. Maggie was there, too. She handed me a brown bag supper—homemade fried chicken, coleslaw, biscuits with honey, and an oatmeal cookie. Together, we sat on a bench by the barn, ate our meal, and watched Liz as she worked with our horse.

"Orphan looks good," I said.

"And it's amazing what this is doing for Liz," Maggie said.

I studied our daughter. She looked wonderful. Healthy. With robust color and a sense of purpose to her life, I'd never seen her better. It seemed inconceivable that she could have been deathly ill just a year earlier.

"Liz's totally focused on that horse," I said.

"She's hoping you'll come and watch her breeze him in the morning."

"What time?"

"Ten o'clock."

"Wouldn't miss it for the world."

In the Texas Panhandle in June, the sun doesn't set until almost nine o'clock. We left Liz to finish her chores and drove back to a gorgeous, burnt-orange display as the huge, round sun slid below the western sky.

At home I found a message from Gus, asking me to call.

"How's it going at Ruidoso Downs?" I asked.

"That's not the question," Gus replied.

"Oh?"

"The question is, how's it going with Orphan?"

"Fine, I guess. I'm going over in the morning to watch Liz breeze him."

"Will you call me as soon as you've seen it?"

"Sure."

"You have a stop watch?" Gus asked

"No."

"Borrow one from Mac. I want you to time him."

CHAPTER 51

Thursday, June 12, TradeWind Airport, Amarillo, Texas

The next morning I did as instructed. Orphan ran 440 yards—a quarter mile, in 22.3 seconds. I asked Mac if that was good.

"Damn good," he replied with a smile."

I called Gus and gave him the time.

"Fantastic," he replied. "Jim Bob, can we use your rig to take Orphan to Ruidoso?"

"Sure," I answered. "When?"

"Tomorrow."

"So soon?"

"We need to get him here so he can adjust to the altitude."

"Okay."

"I'll fly into Tradewind Airport in a charter plane tomorrow morning. Can you pick me up?"

"Sure. What time?"

"Nine o'clock. It's a Beachcraft Bonanza, November 4828 Mike."

"I'll be there."

I walked into the barn and gave Liz a hug. She seemed surprised.

"What was that for?" she asked.

"For a spectacular ride," I said. "And—"

"And what?"

"And Gus is coming tomorrow to take Orphan to Ruidoso."

She looked at me for a moment and turned away. Not before I could see a tear. She pulled off a glove and wiped her face with the back of her hand.

I touched her shoulder. "How about another hug for your daddy?"

She turned and threw her arms around me, the strength of her embrace surprising.

"You've done a great job with Orphan," I said. "Gus could hardly believe me when I told him your breeze this morning was 22.3 seconds."

She eased her grasp. "Got a Kleenex?"

I handed her my handkerchief.

"Thanks." She blew her nose and wiped her eyes. "We knew he was going, just not this soon."

"Liz, we'll travel to Ruidoso every weekend."

She continued to mop her eyes. "This is silly. I'm really happy for Orphan."

"We'll even move there for the entire month of August."

She smiled, a big happy smile. "That'll be nice."

"I'd better go to work." I kissed her on the cheek and left.

As I drove to the clinic, I made a decision. It seemed obvious that I needed to go with Orphan to Ruidoso.

That evening, at the close of the workday, I held another conference with Ida Mae and Fred. Again, I complimented them on the great job they were doing and told them I'd be back after Labor Day.

Ida Mae looked down. I could sense her disappointment. Fred beamed, wishing me well.

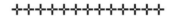

The next morning I stood in front of the tiny airport terminal watching a small blue-and-white, single-engine plane with a distinctive V-tail touch down. It rolled to a stop at the south end of the runway and taxied back. As it came closer I could see two faces, one I recognized. They stopped less than fifty feet away. The door opened and Gus climbed out, walked down the wing, and stepped to the ground. The plane turned around and taxied back out to the runway.

After Gus greeted me with a handshake, we walked another fifty feet to where I had parked my Suburban. In less than twenty seconds we were outside the airport and on the road to his stable.

"That was quick," I said.

"No luggage, no security, no lines," Gus replied. "Pricey, but fast. Flying time was just a little over an hour." He looked at his watch. "What time's the breeze?"

"Mac scheduled it for ten o'clock." I pointed to the digital clock, which showed 9:30. "We'll be there in time for you to help Liz with her saddle."

He grinned. "Listen, at 22.3 seconds, she doesn't need help from me or anyone."

"Tell me about qualifying for the All American," I said. "How do they do it?"

"Scuttlebutt has it that there are 150 two-year-olds at Ruidoso Downs. We'll probably have a few more late arrivals like Orphan. Some will get injured, sick, or just discouraged and quit."

"So if they drop a few and add a few, you think there'll be about 150 horses competing for 10 slots?"

"Yup."

"When are the trials?"

"Monday, August 18. Two weeks before Labor Day."

"I don't understand," I said. "How can they determine the winners in one day?"

"Do the math," Gus replied. "Ten horses in each heat. Fifteen heats will cover it."

"Surely not all in one day?"

"First heat goes at nine a.m. They run one every thirty minutes. If there are fifteen heats, the last one runs at four p.m."

I thought about his answer for a moment.

"They do it by timings," Gus said.

"Oh." I didn't want to expose my ignorance by saying I thought they would take the winner from each heat and have runoffs—a procedure that could last for several days.

Gus continued. "Don't worry. It's all electronic. The same button that opens the gate and rings the bell starts the timers, and they have an infrared beam at the finish line that trips the timer and takes a photograph."

"You're saying it's the ten fastest times, period. Not who wins the heat?"

"You got it."

"Theoretically, the top ten could include several horses from a fast heat?"

"And none from others," Gus replied. "It happens."

"What about Orphan's time? Yesterday I timed him at 22.3 seconds."

"That would have been one of the top ten last year," Gus replied, "but—"

"But what?"

"Too many variables. Condition of the track might be *muddy* or even *sloppy* when the time trials start in the morning. Then the sun comes out and by afternoon it's dried to a condition we call *fast*."

"They have official designations for track conditions?"

"Four," Gus replied. "*Sloppy, Muddy, Poor*, and *Fast*." He chuckled. "Jim Bob, you really don't know much about racing, do you?"

I was too embarrassed to answer.

"And sometimes you'll get a wind shift from nine in the morning to four in the afternoon."

"Wind?"

"Hey, when the timings are in hundredths of a second, the wind can make a big difference."

Our conversation came to an end as we drove up to the barn. Horse training came to a temporary halt. Everyone gathered around to greet Gus, including Liz. Gus hugged her. "The 22.3 rider." he exclaimed.

Liz blushed.

Gus greeted all his employees with a handshake. When he came to Mac, he asked, "You riding in another breeze this morning?"

"In just a few minutes," Mac answered.

Gus, Mac, and I walked out to the starting gate while everyone else went inside the barn to get the horses ready. Mac and Gus talked about the stable. I listened. Mostly the conversation centered on Orphan and how well he was doing.

A few minutes later two horses with riders exited the barn and walked toward us.

"White socks and white blaze," Gus said.

"Say again?" I asked.

"I see where the dyed hairs are just about gone. Orphan has his markings back."

Sure enough, the whiteness around the hooves had returned. When Orphan turned his head in preparation for entering the gate, I could see the characteristic diamond-shaped blaze. It wasn't brilliant white, but the dye was now in its last stages.

Gus took a stopwatch from Mac, then Gus and I walked south to the white flag, which marked a distance of 440 yards. Mac stayed to load the horses.

Orphan went into the gate immediately.

"Look at that," Gus said. "Liz's trained him well."

The other horse resisted. He bucked, kicked, and raised holy hell. Mac grabbed the halter and literally dragged him into the gate. Even after he was in the enclosed area, he reared up, fighting and kicking.

Mac waited, looking for a strategic time to start the race.

Gus tensed, waiting for the exact moment to start his stopwatch.

Time stood still. I found myself afraid to breathe.

Then it happened. The gates flew open to the sound of a clanging bell, and the two horses came barreling toward us. I stepped back a few inches to align myself with Gus' stopwatch and the finish line.

Thundering hooves shook the earth as the two horses passed us. I saw Gus squeeze the stopwatch exactly as Orphan's nose passed our white flag—a full length in front of the other horse.

I turned away from the cloud of dust. When I looked back Gus was grinning ear-to-ear, the biggest, happiest smile I'd ever seen.

"Time?" I asked. "What's the time?"

"You read it," he answered.

I looked. I smiled. It was 21.2 seconds.

Gus slapped me on the back. "That beats the winning time of last year's All American."

CHAPTER 52

U.S. Highway 60, Traveling Southwest From Canyon, Texas,
Toward Ruidoso, New Mexico

After lunch Gus and I loaded Orphan into my cattle trailer, the same rig he'd ridden in as a two-week old foal that memorable day when I first hauled him home from the I-40 wreck. Not the best way to transport a $100,000 racehorse. I vowed to purchase a better trailer just as soon as we won a race. The way things were looking, that might not be too far off.

Thinking Gus knew more about transporting horses on long trips, I asked him if he wanted to drive. He did, and I rode shotgun in the Suburban. He set the cruise control on seventy, and we headed southwest—relaxed in light traffic. Gus in a talkative mood.

"This could be a big year for me," he said as we cruised along.

"Orphan's looking good, isn't he?" I knew the answer, but it seemed a way to keep up my end of the conversation.

"So's Midnight Dash."

"You could have two horses in the All American?"

"Wouldn't that be something?" He grinned.

"Might establish your reputation as a successful trainer," I teased. "You'd be the diva of horseracing."

"What's a diva?"

"That's the best of the best in opera—Liz's dream."

"Is she really that good?" he asked, and I could tell he thought I was just bragging about my kid.

"She's your level only in another field." I watched him closely. "And that's the truth."

He laughed. "I guess singing at the Met is like having one or both of my horses placing in the money."

"Tell me about the money." As he talked, I took out a pad and pencil and started making notes.

"They call this the *Million Dollar Futurity*. At one time it was the richest horserace in the country, bigger even than The Kentucky Derby, The Preakness, or The Belmont."

"So if Orphan wins, we get a million dollars?" I asked.

"Yes, but you have to share it with me, the jockey, and your grooms."

"That's understandable."

"You're required to give 10 percent to the trainer, $100,000, and another $100,000 to the jockey. One percent goes to the head groom—$10,000, and another one percent is split among the top hands that work in the stable. In our case this will be $5,000 each to Rick and Emily—the two assistant grooms."

"So if Orphan wins, we all win?".

"Rest goes to the owner. Seventy-eight percent—$780,000, if Orphan wins."

I smiled and put away the pencil. "I think I could do fine on that amount."

"Before taxes."

"Hey, I've got lots of deductions."

Gus chuckled and drove on down the road.

Three hours later I got my first look at Ruidoso Downs. It was a knockout.

"I could've pulled off the highway a mile back," Gus said, "but I wanted you to see the main entrance—the track and the grandstand."

Located at an elevation of 6,700 feet, with the Rocky Mountains in the background, no racing facility could have a more impressive setting. On that gorgeous afternoon in June, we turned in at the gate, onto a plateau several hundred feet above the beautifully landscaped track. Gus followed the road downhill and circled around the west end of the oval, giving me a full view of a huge grandstand. Flags were everywhere—on top of the stands, around the track, even along the road to the security gate.

Gus showed his credentials to get us into the grounds. We drove about a mile—past the back of the grandstand and the casino—down a long hill to another security gate—this time an entrance into the stables. Gus was on a first name basis with the guards. No credentials needed.

The guards looked in the trailer. "Who's this?" one asked.

"Meet the winner of this year's All American."

The guard laughed. "I've heard that one before. What's its name?"

"Orphan."

Both of the guards laughed. "What a goofy name," one said with a wink as he waved us through the gate.

"What's so funny about Orphan's name?" I asked.

"The tradition in racing is to choose a foal's name as a derivative of its bloodlines. For example, Midnight Dash came from her mother, Blue Midnight, and her father, Dash for the Finish. Her grandfather's name was First Down Dash, and on-and-on. First Down Dash won the All American and set the track record."

"There must be a lot of horses that include *Dash* as part of their name."

"Yup."

"How many horses do you know that have Orphan as part of their name?"

"Yours is the only one, for now."

I looked at Gus, trying to figure his meaning.

He rolled his eyes. "If Orphan wins, I assume you'll offer him for stud."

CHAPTER 53

Ruidoso, New Mexico

Ruidoso Downs, the racetrack corporation, provided stables for all the horses that came to their track—something I didn't know or expect. I guessed they had a hundred or more barns, many of them in poor condition. We had #57, an old, rickety, white-frame building with six stalls, a room for storing feed, and a makeshift office. Located on a muddy lane a quarter-mile east of the track, it wasn't much, but it did supply a roof over our heads and a place to feed and care for our horses. Most importantly, Orphan quickly settled into his stall—a happy home away from home.

Gus had five horses at the track. I knew of three. They were his two stars—Orphan and Midnight Dash—and the old nag, Nellybelle, borrowed from Paul Edwards. Nellybelle's job was to be the *companion horse*, a friend to high-spirited, competitive, and sometimes nervous racers. When we needed a lead horse to ride from our stable out to the racetrack, we rode old Nellybelle.

His other horses were two-year-olds whose chances for the All American were not good, but who might earn some prize money in the weekly races that were held during the summer season.

To look after these five animals, we had a crew of five, in addition to Gus and myself. They included our two riders, Andrea and Robert, and our three grooms. Lupe, the head groom, was in his mid-50s, spoke limited English, and a man with years of experience in tending horses. I noticed that even Gus, whose knowledge I regarded as the ultimate in horsemanship, sometimes deferred to Lupe's judgment. The other two grooms were man and wife, Rick and Emily Brown. I judged them to be in their early twenties, farm kids working their way up in the horse business. Lupe, Rick, and Emily worked hard, really hard, at manning the stable twenty-four hours a day, seven days a week, and would do it from early May until the season closed on Tuesday after Labor Day.

At first, seven people to look after five horses sounded like a lot. I soon learned, at this level, where the competition for a million-dollar race was unbelievably intense, we barely had a skeleton crew.

I pitched in to help muck out the stalls, dispense the medications, review the nutrition plans, and serve as Gus' confidant. He and I took adjoining rooms at a nearby economy motel.

One of the things I found humorous about our arrangement was the way Gus bragged on me. When other trainers visited our stable, he'd introduce me as, "My staff veterinarian." Even the big trainers, like Paul Ray Jones, who brought dozens of horses to New Mexico, didn't have a fulltime DVM at the track.

The arrangement worked both ways. Gus could brag about having a vet, and I learned a lot by just hanging out with him and his staff.

I learned that the racetrack barn becomes your hospital, that "shin-buck" is the most common injury, that others are cherry splints and compression fractures, and I became involved with several

"Thumper Treatments." This is where a vet sends a shockwave of electricity into the shin to move out bad—meaning dead—cells which in turn allows the blood to grow new cells. It takes an expert with patience. The vet's fee is hefty, usually $1,500 or more, an idea I filed away to share with Ida Mae.

The Downs had dozens of vets, and they welcomed me. We often took meals together and almost always, they pumped me about mad cow disease, a problem I had become identified with.

After a week, Gus called a meeting of Lupe, Robert, and me. That was when I learned that Andre had been assigned to ride Midnight Dash and Robert would be Orphan's official jockey.

"We've found an opening in next Saturday's race," Gus said. "What do you think about entering Orphan?"

"He's ready," Robert said. "Let's do it." I could hear youthful exuberance in his words—perhaps too much.

Gus looked at Lupe and me. I knew from his body language, he wanted Orphan to run, but he waited for our opinions. I didn't know what to say.

"Your take, Lupe?" Gus asked.

"Better to wait. Horse will be stronger if you give more time to pick up weight. Also, he only have two weeks at this altitude."

Robert looked disappointed.

"When's the next opening?" I asked.

"That's the problem," Gus replied. "There aren't any. We'll just have to wait for one."

"He needs some experience," Robert argued. "He's the only

horse I know who's not had a race here at The Downs."

I turned to Lupe, "Is that right?"

He nodded. "Most horses been here six weeks and run one race. Some, two."

"What if we run him now, before he's back to full strength and acclimated to the altitude?"

"He won't win," Lupe answered.

"And?"

"Messes a horse's head." He tapped his temple. "Young horses need to feel confidence. Then they run faster."

I turned to Gus. "What Lupe says sounds like good advice to me."

"The problem is," Gus replied, "we may not get another chance before August 18."

"August 18? The time trials?" I asked.

Gus nodded.

The four of us sat there, contemplating the odds.

"Better get some experience," Robert urged.

No one spoke.

"You're the trainer," I said to Gus. "Go with your gut."

"Jockey has point," Lupe interrupted. "Orphan needs to run before time trials."

That was all Gus needed. He'd already decided he wanted Orphan to race.

"I'll do the papers tomorrow morning," he said. "Let's all concentrate on getting him ready."

CHAPTER 54

Ruidoso, New Mexico

Maggie and Liz drove to Ruidoso on Friday. I booked two rooms at a picturesque little bed and breakfast called the Black Bear Inn. Located in the upper canyon, on a winding, narrow road in the mountains above town, it featured a huge wood-burning fireplace, which the owner lit each evening. I took them to dinner at the Cattle Baron's Café, supposedly the premiere steak place in Ruidoso, and we had family time.

The two of them peppered me with questions about Orphan, his training, his adjustment to the altitude, his weight, his health, and most importantly, his timings. I did my best to downplay any optimism. Truthfully, everything looked great, even the timings, but I'd heard so many disappointing stories about first races, about how young horses had been spooked, had stumbled, and had even turned around and run the wrong way. I felt the need to build a layer of caution into their expectations.

Maggie brought up Liz's singing. I jumped at the opportunity to talk about something other than horseracing.

"You practicing?" I asked.

"Every day," Liz answered.

"You have a date for *The Three Sopranos*?"

"Saturday, October 18, Carnegie Hall."

"You couldn't get the Coliseum in Rome?"

"Daaaaaaaad."

"After all, we don't want the tenors to upstage you."

Maggie and I laughed. Liz didn't.

"Listen, you two," she said. "I'm scared to death about walking out on the same stage with big names like Fancher and Griggs. Carnegie Hall would be the world's worst place to make a flop of myself."

I reached over and held her hand. "You're gonna do great."

She squeezed. "And you're a big flatter-er."

I turned loose. "How're you feeling?"

"Fine. Only three more months," she said.

We all knew *the* date—the point at which Dr. Strong had said Liz should be in permanent remission.

"We'll have a family celebration," I said.

"And if Orphan wins, we'll have two things to celebrate."

They brought our steaks.

+++++++++++++

The next morning Liz, Maggie, and I had breakfast at the Inn, a part of the "Bed and Breakfast" arrangement. The homemade blueberry muffins and gourmet coffee were a welcome change, but I couldn't enjoy them. Instead, I picked at my food and worried about the race—about the hundred-and-one things that could go wrong.

ORPHAN

We drove to the stable and parked close to the barn, a long way from our seats in the grandstand—almost a mile. Lupe, had Orphan and Nellybelle exercising on the walker. Maggie recognized old Nellybelle from Orphan's early training days.

"Why are you exercising Orphan with her?" Maggie asked.

"Horses are social animals," I said. "They live in herds, they graze together in the pasture, and they hate to walk alone. Orphan does better on the walker if Nellybelle walks with him." I took my wife's hand and held it.

"You're so smart," Maggie said.

"I picked that up last week from Lupe," I replied.

Gerald McCastland, the assistant trainer from Gus' Canyon Stable, greeted us, and we learned that he had driven down the night before to see Orphan's first race.

"I hear you have an empty seat in your box," Mac said.

"Mac," I replied, "you know more about the arrangements than we do. If you say we have room, we'd love to have someone with us who knows the way."

Mac had a club-cab pickup. He got Lupe to drive us to the grandstand.

Chapter 55

The Grandstand, Ruidoso Downs

The Grandstand, Ruidoso Downs

Race day anywhere is exciting. For thousands of summertime racing fans, Ruidoso is more so because of the mountains, the smell of the pines, the storied history of the racetrack—the ambiance that accompanies the home of the All American Futurity. Like watching golf at Augusta National in April, or baseball in Yankee Stadium during the World Series, attending Saturday afternoon races at this special place was guaranteed to heighten one's interest and cause a horseracing fan's blood pressure to rise.

This sense of excitement was amplified exponentially for a select group of people—the owners of the horses. Ten races, ten horses in each race, brought more than one hundred owners, co-owners, and their families. These individuals came to the grandstand with their adrenaline pumping at record levels. Years of planning and training—not to mention considerable financial investment—were on the line.

The peak of anxiety belonged to people like me and my family—*new* owners attending the first race of their horse. I was so wired I could hardly stand it. Thank heavens the racetrack provided special accommodations for us.

Mac knew the way. He used our owners' passes to get Liz, Maggie, and me onto an elevator for the "owners level," a mezzanine floor above the regular grandstand seats. There, we found special seating—boxes with spacious chairs—and a bird's-eye view of the track. Our four seats were on the front row not far from the finish line.

An added perk was the private restaurant. Located behind the owners' boxes, toward the back of the grandstand, we found an area about fifty feet wide that ran the entire length of the mezzanine. This space contained tables and chairs for dining. While the view was somewhat less ideal than the front row boxes, owners could enjoy food and drink while sitting at these tables, and watching the races. Also available on this level were special, plush betting booths, and restrooms.

Races started at twelve o'clock and continued throughout the afternoon, usually a race every twenty minutes. Orphan was in the ninth race. I calculated that it would be at about 2:40 p.m. However, Gus cautioned me that the schedule often ran late, and it was more likely Orphan's race would occur sometime between three and four.

We settled in and waited for the first race. The box on our right contained a family from Fort Worth. On the left, a group of four elderly ladies—a partnership—owned a horse from California.

Exactly at noon we heard the familiar trumpet followed by the announcer's lengthy spiel about the first race. As the horses paraded past the grandstand on their way to the gates, the ladies on our left became more animated. One of them turned to Maggie.

"That's our horse," she said. "Number four."

I looked in my program to see that his name was "Blinding Speed," owned by a syndicate in northern San Diego County called "The Bridge Club." From their appearance, I guessed the youngest to be seventy-five, if she was a day.

A large electronic board facing the grandstand gave information about the race. Some of it, such as the names and numbers of the horses, I readily understood, but I turned to the family seated on my right to ask about the other numbers.

"Those are the odds," the man replied with a smile.

"Horse number four—the board says seventeen to one."

"Yes, you bet one dollar to win, and if he does, you get seventeen."

"So his chances aren't good?"

"He's a long shot."

I thanked him and continued to read about the others until I heard the ringing of a bell, and the announcer's voice, "They're off. Wicked Lady is in the lead, Classy Lad second, Vodka on Ice and Firestorm Pete are neck and neck for third." He continued his announcing at such a rapid pace I could barely understand him. Twenty-three seconds later, it was over. Blinding Speed came in last.

The scoreboard listed the winners—first, second, and third places—and their odds.

Maggie did her best to console the ladies.

The next four races went much the same. The horse owned by the family on our right ran in the fifth race and came in second. They seemed happy. I hardly remember races six, seven, and eight.

Then they brought out ten horses for the ninth race. Orphan was number three and his odds were posted on the board as four to one.

ORPHAN

The program listed him as a promising unknown in his first race, a latecomer, but not in tip-top shape. We watched a quarter-mile away as they loaded horses into the gate. Numbers one and six went first. Then two and seven. Next they loaded Orphan and number eight. We waited as they loaded four and nine, and finally numbers five and ten. I could feel my heart pounding.

The bell rang and it looked to me as though Orphan had a good break. I heard the announcer say number three was in the lead followed by seven and two. On the next call number three had opened his lead to a length. When they whizzed by me, closing to the finish line, Orphan was two full lengths ahead.

The announcer went ballistic.

CHAPTER 56

Ruidoso Downs, The Winner's Circle, down by the track

Mac led the way, not waiting for the elevator. We followed him down two flights of stairs and into a tunnel under the racetrack. At the end of the passageway, we ran up the steps and over to the Winner's Circle.

As we hurried through the crowd, we could hear the announcer rattling on, "No horse wins by two lengths in these short, quarter-mile races." Orphan did, and the time was 21.212 seconds, almost a tenth of a second off the track record. When a new track record was announced, the crowd came to their feet, clapping and cheering.

We found Gus at the Winner's Circle. Robert, our jockey, was jumping up and down—almost crazy with excitement. A woman from the racetrack's PR department arranged us for a photograph—owners on one side of the horse, trainer and jockey on the other. Flashguns started going off like a July Fourth celebration. In the confusion, no one thought to hold on to Orphan's halter.

The first flash made him skittish. He reared up, pulling the reins from Liz's hands.

ORPHAN

Multiple flashes blinded us.

Orphan bolted.

Before anyone could move, he had jumped the rail and was back out on the racetrack. Gus, Mac, and I ran after him. Someone screamed. Shouts from the grandstand made it worse. Our scared, two-year-old ran toward the only place he knew—the stables.

Ahead I saw him leave the racetrack and head downhill toward a line of horses coming this way for the next race. He dodged them. In so doing, he ended up on the street with cars trying to get out of his way.

The street was blacktop. The blacktop was slick. When Orphan hit the slick surface and tried to swerve to avoid traffic, he slipped.

When I saw it, I cringed.

He looked like Bambi on ice. First one leg went out, then the others—seemingly in all different directions. When he went down I could hear the sound, a big splat. He struggled to get up. Then in horror, I watched him try to go on—limping. He was holding his left front leg up off the ground as he attempted to hobble his way back toward our stable.

CHAPTER 57

Ruidoso Veterinary Services

We took Orphan to a clinic with an equine X-ray machine. Two DVMs—specialists in horse leg injuries—showed Gus and me huge negatives on state-of-the-art equipment. The more I conversed with these guys, the more I realized how fortunate we were. Orphan was at one of the world's best facilities for orthopedic horse treatment.

Using an endoscope—a tiny medical camera inserted into the body through a small incision—the doctors found where Orphan had chipped his knee. Arthroscopic surgery followed immediately. We watched as they removed the chip, a tiny sliver of bone so small I thought it a miracle they found it all. If we were lucky—if we somehow managed to avoid infection or other complications—recovery would be four to six weeks.

They removed the bone fragment on June 28.

Time trials for the big race were August 18.

We had seven weeks.

Maggie and Liz decided to stay in Ruidoso and help. Good thing. They became indispensable members of Orphan's four-person recovery team. I took charge of the medical. Gus directed physical conditioning. Maggie and Liz had responsibility for his therapy.

Each morning I scrubbed his knee and applied topical medications to make the leg sweat. Liz followed with leg wrappings, the first of many throughout the day. Then Maggie attached ice packs, an essential part of my hot-and-cold therapy. During the first week Orphan appeared to be healing nicely. I thought things were going well.

Gus didn't. "Jim Bob, he's losing muscle tone."

"Obviously," I replied. "If he's not able to exercise, what'd you expect?"

Gus ignored my question. "It won't matter if his leg heals perfectly if the result is an athlete that's out of shape."

"You know we have to give that knee time to heal."

"How about swimming?"

"What about it?"

"Ruidoso has an Aqua-tread," Gus replied. "It's a big tank filled with warm water that has a treadmill on the floor."

I thought about it. "Water flotation would reduce the weight-bearing demands on his knee?"

Gus nodded. "Exactly."

"Let me look into it."

Gus didn't like my answer. I didn't like his pushing me. We went our separate ways. He worked on his other horses. I stewed about what to do with mine.

The next day I called on the two orthopedic guys who'd performed Orphan's surgery and asked their advice. One cautioned me against it because of the risk of infection. The other gave me ambivalent counsel—might help, probably wouldn't, try it and see.

That afternoon Gus and I went to look at the Aqua-tread. It was huge, and expensive.

Gus pushed. "Jim Bob, we've got to find some way to exercise him. If we don't do this, the only alternative is to take him out on the track."

That did it. I signed us up for the Aqua-tread—once a day, an hour in the late afternoon. At five o'clock we took Orphan swimming.

Liz got into the tank with him. We started slowly, only fifteen minutes at a slow walk. Not much more than what he was doing in his stall. When he got out, Liz gave him some apple slices.

The next day went even better, and we did twenty minutes. Again, more apple slices.

Over the week we continued to add five minutes each day until we were up to an hour's workout. I checked his knee three times a day, first thing each morning, the last each night, and always at the Aqua-tread, what we laughingly called the swimming pool. No swelling. No sign of infection. No symptoms of any kind.

At the beginning of the second week, we signed for two swims a day.

Liz went to the grocery store and bought apples by the bushel.

By the end of our second week—the third week since the fall— Gus was smiling again.

"When do you think we can start walking on the track?" he asked.

"Gus, give his knee a chance," I pleaded.

"The time trials are four weeks from tomorrow."

"And he's doing great."

"All the other horses are galloping, breezing, and entering races."

"All the other horses who've had knee surgery?"

Gus scowled, shook his head, and stomped off.

The next day I loaded Orphan in my trailer and took him back to Ruidoso Veterinary Services for an evaluation of the knee. Both vets patted him down—a manual examination of his injury. Next they took a series of X-rays. Then the three of us studied the negatives.

"Looking good," said one.

"You've done a nice job with his therapy," added the other. "No hint of trauma. No sign of any complications."

"My trainer's anxious to build Orphan's physical strength. He wants to start walking next week, light galloping the following week, and run some breezes the week before the time trials."

The first vet laughed. "What else is new?"

"Trainers are always pushing the envelope," the second one said.

"He'll heal faster and better if you wait."

"On the other hand, if he's not in shape, he can't win—in a highly competitive race."

I thought about their comments for a moment. "It doesn't get any more competitive than the time trials for the All American."

The first vet shrugged. "You make your choice and don't look back."

Chapter 58

Ruidoso Downs

Living in the mountains in the summer should be a happy time. The smell of the pines, cool nights, bright early morning sunshine, frequent late afternoon showers—I should have been one of those cheerful people who came to this resort area to enjoy horseracing. Instead, all I did was worry.

Gus worried, too, so we compromised. I eased up on my medical restrictions. He scaled back on his training requirements.

On Monday, three weeks before the time trials, we started walking Orphan. Gus decided to "pony" him—an arrangement where Gus rode a lead horse, tied a rope to Orphan's halter, and led him for his walk. The first day entailed a short distance at a slow pace. On each succeeding day, they pushed for a little more distance and speed.

The next week Gus added a light gallop with Orphan still on a lead rope. Each day they galloped a bit farther and faster. On day six, Gus asked Robert, the jockey, to ride Orphan. With Gus on old Nellybelle and Robert on Orphan, they went out to gallop around the track. Liz, Maggie, and I watched. Orphan looked good.

One week before time trials, Gus added a breeze. We took two horses out to the gate—Robert rode Orphan, and Andrea, our other jockey, rode Midnight Dash. Gus and I watched from a point 440 yards away. This was the first time since the accident we'd allowed Orphan to run from the gate. No stopwatch. This was supposed to be an easy race.

Lupe loaded the two horses, raised his right hand—the one with the start button—a signal to us that he was ready. I tensed. Three things happened simultaneously—Lupe swung his hand down, we heard the bell, and the gates flew open. Gus had planned this to be a breeze, the two horses running at an easy pace. It was anything but.

Midnight leaped out of the gate at full speed. Through my binoculars I could see the filly's muscles flexing with Andrea, her jockey, leaning forward—hanging on. Gus had given Robert strict instructions about not pushing Orphan. This was a *training race*, an exercise for a horse with a *leg that was healing,* The problem was, no one had told Orphan or Midnight Dash, and they were two of the most competitive horses at the track.

As they passed the 220 mark, I lowered the binoculars and let my naked eyes take in the drama. Midnight had come out of the gate slightly in front. Orphan strained, and, by the 330 mark, had a nose in front. Then, with a heavy heart, I watched as he faded. Midnight Dash pulled away. The filly was in better shape and won by a head.

The two horses thundered past and began to slow. With both jockeys standing in their stirrups, they came to a stop, turned, and started walking back to where we were standing. Gus was angrier than I'd ever seen him.

"I told you not to push him," Gus yelled at Robert.

Orphan's jockey swung down out of the saddle. "I didn't."

"That knee is still healing," Gus shouted, his voice cutting. "You may have injured it."

"Gus, I wasn't doing anything to urge him on. This is a horse that wants to run."

Gus knelt by the leg and felt it, running his hands up and down the knee.

"How does it feel?" I asked.

"I can't tell," he replied.

"He's not limping or showing any signs of favoring the injury."

"Yeah, but let's see how he's doing tomorrow morning."

I backed away. Gus stood. Robert, still reeling from Gus' stinging criticism, led Orphan toward the stables.

Ahead of us, about fifty yards, I could see Andrea holding the reins to Midnight Dash. She led the horse toward a group of men standing near the gate, the entrance to the stables. At first I didn't pay much attention to what she was doing, but my eye caught a tall man with a short black beard. At that distance he looked like Edgar Payne.

Andrea stopped at the gate. The horse came between me and the group of men who gathered around to admire the winner of the breeze.

Robert continued on with Orphan, through the gate, toward the stable.

I followed.

Gus joined the group admiring Midnight Dash.

A familiar voice boomed out congratulations. "Gus, I told you Midnight would become the faster horse."

I hurried to catch up with Orphan, but out of the corner of my eye I saw Gus shake Edgar Payne's hand.

Chapter 59

Barn #57, Ruidoso Downs

I felt betrayed. Ten minutes later, when Gus returned to the barn, I confronted him, "Whose side are you on?" I snarled, making no attempt to hide my anger.

"I'm on the side of all my horses," Gus replied. "You know that we have four horses here. I'm doing my best for four different owners, you included."

"Edgar Payne is one of your owners?"

"He's head of the syndicate that owns Midnight."

Gus' news flabbergasted me. For a moment I couldn't think. "Why didn't you tell me?"

"It was part of the deal," Gus answered, not meeting me eye-to-eye. "Last April, just before you left to take your daughter to New York, Payne came to see me."

"Yes, I remember."

"He came to tell me that Futurity Stables had purchased the controlling interest in Midnight. He asked me if I would like to continue as trainer. I said I would. He added. . ." Gus looked up, and we

257

locked eyes. "Payne said he wouldn't hire me as trainer unless I agreed to keep the change of ownership quiet."

"Gus, that's dishonest."

"Let me ask you a question," he said. "Do you need to know who the owners are of the other two horses here in this barn, the other horses I'm training? Do you even care?"

"That's different," I replied.

"How's it different?"

"There's something about Payne. He's probably dishonest."

"Probably?"

"And he's accused of murdering Anna Garcia."

"He's been indicted?"

"Well, no."

Gus raised his shoulders and held out his hands, palms up. "I rest my case."

"He has a violent temper," I countered. "I've seen him when he lashes out. I think he's capable of anything—even murder."

"You think?"

"Yes."

"Want me to tell you what I think?"

I wanted to say, no. I wanted to tell Gus he was wrong, dead wrong. I wanted to tell him I thought Payne was a liar, a cunning schemer, a probable murderer, and the person I thought had stolen Orphan. I didn't. Instead, I shook my head. I could see it was useless. I responded with the only word I could think of, "Okay."

"I think he's a hard-working, smart guy," Gus said. "I admit I've not seen him often, but all of his dealings with me have been honest and forthright. He pays his bills on time, and he treats me fair."

"Wait until you cross him."

"There's no need to cross him."

"Give it time," I warned.

I saw the discussion was going nowhere. Gus looked disgusted, and I was only getting angrier. To cool us both down, I changed the subject, "Okay, let's forget about Payne for the moment. How's Orphan?"

Gus grudgingly relented. "Don't know. If he's re-injured the knee, we'll have to deal with it in the morning."

Gus turned and walked away. I felt as though a thick, glass wall had risen between us.

CHAPTER 60

The Ruidoso Time Trials

The day of reckoning dawned bright, cool, and with a fast track. It hadn't rained in the past twenty-four hours, and weather forecasters predicted no precipitation for the day. Perfect conditions.

I met Gus at the barn at 4:30 a.m. He gathered the grooms around and lectured us. Gerald McCastland, who had driven down from Amarillo, also joined us.

"Horses like routine," Gus said. "We need to make this day as much like a normal day as possible."

Lupe nodded.

"Do not act nervous," Mac added. "If the horses sense we are nervous, they become nervous too. One of the worst things that could happen today is for our horses to develop a case of nerves."

The four horses in Gus' stable were spaced out in the time trials. The first, a gelding, scheduled in the third heat at ten o'clock, did not do well. We hadn't expected much, so no one reacted. Besides, he'd placed in a couple of summer races and earned enough to pay for his expenses. The absentee owners lived in Iowa and would be pleased.

Midnight Dash ran at 12:30 in heat number eight and won by a length. When any horse wins by that much, it creates a buzz. Midnight's time was 21.246 seconds, the third fastest time so far in the trials. The filly seemed assured of a place in the big race. When Edgar Payne and his buddies came to the barn to congratulate Gus, the jockey, and the grooms, I ducked out the rear door.

After lunch I came back in time to see the third horse saddled up and led away to the three o'clock heat. No one thought he had a chance, and sure enough, he came in last in the group—his timing of 24.517 ranked tenth from the bottom of all horses who had run during the day. I didn't know the owners and Gus didn't tell me their names. No one showed to check on their horse, and I learned an important fact about horses and their owners. A loser doesn't have much of a following.

We heard the trumpet for the fourteenth race, which ran at four o'clock. It told us we had thirty minutes to get Orphan ready and walk him to the racetrack. The pace picked up in our barn as Gus, Robert, and the grooms saddled our horse and made last-minute preparations.

"Mind if I sit with you, again?" Mac asked.

"Sure," I replied.

This time Maggie, Liz, and I knew the routine, and even though this wasn't a race, it functioned like one. The stakes for owners were much greater. Emily, one of our grooms, drove Mac's pickup and let us out at the main entrance to the grandstand. Again, we followed Mac to the elevator, and took our places in the front row of the owners' mezzanine. We watched as they led the horses for the fifteenth heat into the paddock. Again, Orphan was number three and, just like a race, the horses paraded in front of the grandstand on their way to the starting gate.

I used my binoculars to watch the preparations. As usual, they loaded gates one and six, then two and seven. Orphan came into the third gate with no problems, as did number eight, but the horse in gate four went crazy. He bucked and kicked, making it impossible to continue. The loading process, normally a one or two-minute operation, dragged on interminably. I have no idea how long we waited, but the frustration grew. Finally, when the horse in gate four injured himself, race officials announced a ten-minute delay and all the horses were taken out of the gates.

The next announcement told us that horse number four had withdrawn from competition due to injuries, and the fifteenth heat would have only nine horses. Race handlers restarted the loading of the gates. A minute later came the familiar ringing of the bell, the opening of the gates, and the announcer's excited voice, "They're off."

At the first call, 220 yards, Orphan led by a head.

At the second call, 330 yards, he was ahead by a length.

At the finish line, he won by a length and a half.

We were ecstatic. The old Orphan was back, and his time of 21.213 was 33/1000 of a second better than Midnight Dash. Our horse was the new third-best of all the time trials. Liz, Maggie, and I danced, hugged, and generally went crazy. Dozens of people in the owners' mezzanine congratulated us, shook our hands, and stood around smiling.

Mac shared in the good news, shaking hands, and accepting congratulations for us.

People came for the sixteenth heat, the last of the day, and asked for our seats. Mac led as we walked the long way back to barn #57.

ORPHAN

We followed—a happy time—as we found a party in progress.

Gus brought glasses and a bottle of champagne. Mac poured. Liz, Maggie, and I joined Gus, Mac, and some others I didn't know, in a toast. It was the first time I could ever remember drinking Dom Perignon to the smell of horseshit.

CHAPTER 61

Ruidoso Downs, Barn #57

The next day Gus and I examined Orphan carefully. We agreed that the knee looked normal. Gus suggested we escalate our training regimen, and I concurred. No more swimming. Physical stamina would be the goal. We brought Lupe and Robert into our planning, and the four of us mapped out a gradual, six-day increase in exercise.

After Lupe and Robert left, Gus poured two cups of coffee, and we took a couple of chairs at his desk. I tried to think of ways to rebuild the trust between Gus and myself, so I asked him about the purse, the way the prize money is paid to the ten horses in the big race.

"The purse is capped at two million dollars," he said.

"Capped?" I asked.

"In the early years, those immediately after World War IJ, the race returns increased every year and the prize money escalated with it. Then about twenty years ago—when First Place reached one million dollars, and it had become the richest purse in horseracing—the racetrack owners decided to cap the purse so future increases in profits could be used to build incentives for the races for older horses."

"But you said it's capped at two million? If first place takes one million, what happens to the second million?"

Gus opened his briefcase and rummaged through a stack of papers. He pulled out a tattered sheet with worn edges, obviously a document that had been studied many times. He handed it to me.

PURSE FOR THE ALL AMERICAN (capped at $2,000,000.00)

1ST PLACE	*$1,000,000 (50%)*
2ND PLACE	*$300,000 (15%)*
3RD PLACE	*$157,750 (7.89%)*
4TH PLACE	*$125,200 (6.26%)*
5TH PLACE	*$100,250 (5%)*
6TH PLACE	*$85,500 (4.28%)*
7TH PLACE	*$67,000 (3.35%)*
8TH PLACE	*$64,300 (3.22%)*
9TH PLACE	*$50,000 (2.5%)*
10TH PLACE	*$50,000 (2.5%)*

I studied it with great interest. "So you're telling me I've already won $50,000?"

He smiled. "I think everyone's expecting you'll follow the percentages stipulated by Ruidoso Downs and share it with your trainer, jockey, and grooms."

"Of course, and that means if your two horses come in ninth and tenth, you've won 5 percent of each—$10,000."

"How much for first and second?" he asked.

I did the easy math. "$130,000."

He laughed, "Just so you'll know, it's never happened that one trainer has won both first and second."

"Now who's being pessimistic?"

We both laughed and it felt good. The glass wall that had been between us for the last few days appeared to have shattered.

Lupe came to the door, a worried look on his face. "You both must come look at Orphan. He sick."

CHAPTER 62

Ruidoso Downs, Barn #57

"What do you mean, sick?" Gus asked.

"You come look," Lupe said, again.

Gus and I followed Lupe the length of the barn to the last stall. There was no particular reason why we had chosen this one for Orphan except that he was the last horse to arrive, and at the time it had been empty. Whatever. The seven of us—three grooms, two riders, Gus, and I—called it Orphan's stall and, for the summer, it had been his home.

Lupe opened the door.

Gus went in, stood next to the horse, rubbed his neck, and spoke to him in a soft, calm voice.

Standing at the door, I watched, trying to look for clues.

After a few moments, Gus backed away to the far corner and then slowly walked around the perimeter of the room, studying Orphan.

Our horse stood there with his head down, lifeless.

"Something's wrong," I said. "I've never seen him hang his

head like that."

"And he's sweating," Gus said, "for no apparent reason."

"Maybe Founder?" Lupe asked. "He acts like stomach hurts."

Gus came close and again rubbed Orphan's neck. Then, one at a time, he picked up each hoof and examined it. "Founder mainly comes from feeding too much grain, too much protein. It also affects the feet—makes them sore."

The three of us walked back outside the stall and closed the door.

"I measure grain, myself," Lupe said, his voice agitated, defensive. "It's what you have on wall." He pointed to Gus' instructions written with a magic marker on a whiteboard to the left of the door. I scanned it while Lupe was talking and saw that it was exactly what our Miami vet had prescribed.

"Lupe, no one's accusing you," Gus replied. "And Orphan's feet look perfectly normal. It's not founder."

The three of us stood there for several minutes, silently pondering Orphan's symptoms.

"Let's give it twenty-four hours," I said. "Maybe it'll correct itself."

Gus shook his head. "That's wishful thinking, but I can't come up with anything else right now."

"How about we do a round-the-clock watch?" I suggested. "Take turns having someone here by the door."

Gus liked the idea. "Lupe, I want you to organize six-hour shifts. Make sure one of us is here night and day until we figure out what's causing this."

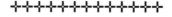

The next morning Orphan acted worse, not better. His gallop was lethargic and, back in his stall, he continued to hang his head. On my own initiative I began a one-man investigation of everything that went into our horse's stomach. I found something in the most unlikely of places—Orphan's hay.

At first glance his alfalfa looked perfectly normal. It was only by accident—I had pulled down the feeding net by the door and spread the hay on the floor, looking for foreign objects—that I found it. There was nothing foreign. What I found instead was a fairly sizable batch of gray-and-black fibers—moldy hay that had turned bad through natural deterioration. The only suspicious aspect of my finding was the way it had been concealed.

I wrapped it back with the good, leafy, greenish hay on the outside and re-hung the net. Then I continued to search our barn for the next hour before asking Gus to walk with me to Orphan's stall.

"Who fills the nets with hay?" I asked.

He shrugged. "The grooms, mostly, sometimes others. Why do you ask?"

I pointed to the hay net. "See anything wrong?"

He looked, shook his head. "You trying to say Orphan's not eating enough hay?"

"Guess again." I pulled down the net and scattered its contents on the floor for him to see.

His eyes grew big with revulsion. "Damn."

"I've examined all the hay bales in our storage room. I've also looked at every one of the other horses' hay nets. All our hay is top-grade, fresh alfalfa."

"Except this?"

I nodded. "Someone's deliberately trying to make Orphan sick."

"And succeeding."

A brief silence hung in the air as Gus realized the implications.

"It's one of us," Gus murmured.

"Has to be."

I've seen Gus mad, but never like this. An ugly scowl came over his face, and he stomped around, ready to explode. He opened his mouth several times, but nothing came out.

"I have a suggestion," I said.

"What?" Gus snarled.

"We need to go slow."

"Why in God's name would you do that?" he yelled. "Let's nail the bastard."

"I think we have to catch him, or her, in the act," I replied, "otherwise everyone will probably have an alibi, and we'll never find out who it is."

"Jim Bob, we don't have time to mess around."

"I think this may be the fastest way to bring an end to our problem."

I outlined a surveillance plan where Liz, Maggie, Gus, and I would take four-hour shifts watching with binoculars from the roof of barn #56, the building across the road. From fifty yards away, it offered a perfect view of the stall on the end.

Orphan's stall.

CHAPTER 63

Ruidoso Downs, Barn #57

Maggie agreed to take the first watch—four o'clock to eight.

Liz came next and stayed until midnight.

I relieved her and took my place on the roof. It seemed ridiculous to have double surveillance—our staff watching the horse and my family watching the staff, but I couldn't think of any other way to resolve our dilemma.

Robert was on duty. Using my binoculars, I watched him as he sat in a chair by the door to the stall, reading. Of all the staff, I thought Robert the least likely to bring harm to our horse. As jockey, he was close to Orphan and had personal motives for success. If we did well in the race, he would receive celebrity status and—other than Gus or myself—the largest share of the purse. By 2:00 a.m., this seemed like a huge waste of time.

I shifted and tried to find a more comfortable position. I put the glasses aside and decided to watch with my naked eyes. While I couldn't see much detail from a distance of fifty yards, it was enough to observe Robert sitting in a chair. I had a hard time staying awake and imagined that he, too, might be napping.

Then Robert stood. I grabbed the binoculars. He took down the net with hay and walked the entire length of the barn to his car, which was parked in front. He opened the trunk, shielding himself from my view, and did something for four or five minutes.

I called Gus on my cellphone, reported our situation, and asked him to bring Ruidoso Downs security.

Robert carried the hay net back to the stall and hung it by the door. I thought he would return to his chair—maybe take a nap. He didn't. Instead, he got a bucket and filled it with water.

I called Gus' cell. "Where are you?"

"I'm at the gate," he answered. "The security guys are waiting for the police."

"Robert is doing something with the water. I think you should come now and try to catch him by surprise."

"Be there in a couple of minutes."

I left my post—probably both dumb and dangerous—but I wanted to find out what was in the water. As quietly and quickly as I could, I slipped over to the back door. Peering around the corner, I saw Robert bent over the pail dumping something into it. He used a stick to stir the liquid. Then he stood, stuffed a prescription bottle back into his pocket, and reached for the latch to Orphan's stall. I was about ten feet away.

"Hi, Robert," I said as I walked around the corner.

The look on his face said it all.

"How's Orphan doing?" I asked.

"Just . . . just fine," he replied.

"Here, let me help you." I picked up the bucket and walked into Orphan's stall.

Robert looked bewildered. He stood there with his mouth open.

"Maybe we should empty the old water and make room for the fresh?" I nodded to the blue plastic tub in the corner.

"Uh . . . yes . . . that's what we usually do," he replied. He reached to dump the water.

"Robert, that'll make the stall muddy," I cautioned. "Better if you empty it outside."

He looked at me for a moment, unsure of what to do.

I gestured with my head toward the door.

With considerable hesitation, he lifted Orphan's drinking tub and started out.

At the doorway he ran into Gus and a racetrack security officer. The security guy had his gun drawn. Gus grabbed the blue plastic tub.

In the distance we heard a siren.

The next few minutes came in a rush.

Police handcuffed Robert without any fuss. They impounded his car which had moldy hay in the trunk. The racetrack security officer took three incriminating pieces of evidence—a prescription bottle of pills from Robert's pocket, the bucket of water I was holding, and Orphan's blue tub of water.

Police led Robert away. Gus and I followed them to Ruidoso Headquarters where we signed a complaint accusing Robert of drugging our horse.

I started the drive back to Black Bear Lodge and looked at my watch. It was 3:30 a.m.

CHAPTER 64

Ruidoso Downs, Barn #57

The next morning, for the first time since the time trials, Orphan looked better.

Gus looked worse.

"We've turned the corner," I said. "Things are looking up."

"No jockey," Gus replied, "and the All American is only six days away."

"Get another jockey." The answer seemed obvious to me.

"Andrea's riding Midnight."

"There must be a hundred jockeys here at the racetrack who'd love to have a ride in the big race."

"Not that many, and of those, none are familiar with our horse."

I flashed a big smile. "You want me to go hire us a jockey?" I thought he would see immediately that I was kidding. He didn't.

"You wouldn't know the first thing about hiring a jockey."

Which was true, and I could see that Gus was in no mood for kidding around. "Let me take care of the stable today. You go find a jockey that can win the race."

After Gus left, I gathered Rick, Emily, Lupe—and Andrea, our only jockey, for a conference. "Gus is out trying to find someone to replace Robert. It's up to us to carry on."

"You still want us to guard the stable twenty-four hours a day?" Lupe asked.

"No. Maggie, Liz, and I will take over the security."

"Who's going to exercise Orphan?" Andrea asked.

"I know it means extra work, but until we get another jockey, you'll have to exercise both Midnight and Orphan."

She nodded. "Sure."

"The race is only five days away," I said. "We have two magnificent horses, probably the two best in the race. This is a great opportunity for us. We need to concentrate on winning—on taking care of our horses—and try to forget about Robert."

"We know what to do," Lupe said.

"I'll get Midnight ready for galloping," Emily said.

Rick nodded. "And I'll have Orphan saddled and ready when you get back."

The troops went to work and I felt a renewed sense of purpose. We'd found the source of Orphan's illness. We still had a chance. I had high hopes that Gus would find us a good jockey, that Orphan would recover quickly, and that we'd be back in contention.

Lupe and I mucked out the stalls, spreading fresh straw and sawdust, getting our routine back to normal.

Liz and Maggie brought a pizza for lunch, and the three of us planned a new security schedule. We decided on eight-hour shifts—Maggie four to midnight, Liz midnight to eight o'clock the next morning, and I'd take the day shift.

Andrea got ready to give our two horses a strong workout that afternoon. I followed her out to the track to watch. Midnight looked great, in top form. Orphan seemed lethargic and sluggish.

After the exercise runs, the grooms hosed down the horses, put them on the walker, and gave them their afternoon feedings.

Andrea and I went to the office and talked about our plans for the next day.

"Where's Gus?" she asked.

"Haven't seen him," I replied. "He must be working really hard to find a new jockey."

"After tomorrow, there're only four days to get ready."

"He knows that."

"It's not good for a horse to enter a race with a strange rider," she said.

"Especially the All American," I replied. "You know any good jockeys?"

She looked startled. "Why are you asking me? That's Gus' job."

I could see this was not a suitable topic and tried to change the subject. "Have you seen Midnight's owner?"

"Mr. Payne?"

"I wonder why he's not around. All the other owners who have a horse in the big race, come by to check on things."

"Yeah. That *is* unusual," she said, "but when I talked to him after the time trials, he made a special point of telling me he had to go to Albuquerque and wouldn't see me until the day of the race."

"Strange."

She nodded. "He didn't say it, but I got the impression that part of the reason he stays away is you."

"Me?"

"He knows you're here working with your horse."

I thought about Andrea's comment. Maybe she had him figured out. "You have any problems with Payne?"

"None. He's been great to work with, so far."

"Ever seen him lose his temper?"

"Nope," Andrea replied. "There's never been anything for him to get mad about. Midnight's doing fine. Why do you ask?"

I wanted to warn her, to alert her to the other side of his persona. I thought about how to phrase my words. There didn't seem to be any way to tell her about Payne's behavior without bad-mouthing him. For a brief moment I studied her face and her body language, and then changed my mind. "If you're getting along with him, I think I should stay out of it."

"All I know is, he has a great horse and I get to ride her."

I tried switching the subject, "Wonder if Gus has hired a jockey?"

She shrugged and looked at her watch. "Dr. Masterson, I'm beat. Okay if I call it a day?"

"Jim Bob." I smiled. "Call me Jim Bob, and yes, you need to get your rest. These next five days are going to be big ones for you and for me."

"Hey, we can't count Labor Day. There are only four days for training."

She left.

Maggie and I checked on the horses.

Gus finally showed up with a sack of hamburgers. The three of us ate in his office. Maggie and I listened while he talked about his search.

"Every jockey I talked with wants to ride Orphan," Gus said.

"Great. Then our problem's easily solved," I said between bites.

"Did you hire one?" Maggie asked.

"No. I wanted to check with the trainers they listed as references."

"And?"

"Trainers are hard to find. Many left after their horses didn't qualify. Most of those who are still here in Ruidoso won't answer their cellphones."

"So what've you got?" I asked.

He opened his briefcase and pulled out a legal pad. "Five names that look promising."

I looked at his scribbling. Twice as many names had been crossed off. "What's wrong with these?"

"Drugs, alcohol, mean spirited—you name it. Remember, I'm talking with trainers who didn't win. The trainer always blames the jockey."

There didn't seem to be any point to continuing the conversation. I left Maggie in charge of security. Gus got on the phone to call more references. I went back to the Black Bear Inn, hoping for a better day, and fell asleep the instant my head touched the pillow.

It seemed like only seconds later the phone woke me.

It rang several times while I struggled to find the light switch. As I reached for the receiver I looked at my wristwatch—12:15 a.m.

"Hello," I said.

"Dad, we need you," Liz said.

"What's wrong?"

"Gus is dead."

CHAPTER 65

The Black Bear Bed abnd Breakfast

I sat up, now wide awake.

"Dead?" I whispered, fearing if I said the word too loud it might be true.

"He . . . isn't breathing," Liz must have been shaking violently, her words came out in hiccups. "We . . . can't find . . . a pulse. I called 911."

"Where are you?"

"Here in the office . . . with Mom."

I wedged the phone between my chin and my shoulder as I fumbled for my clothes. "Okay, honey. Calm down. Tell me what happened."

"I got to the barn at midnight to relieve Mom." The pitch of Liz's voice leveled as she talked. "We noticed that Gus had passed out, his head on the desk. At first we thought he was asleep, but when we tried to wake him, he felt cold, wasn't breathing—" Her voice broke. "No . . . no pulse."

I could hear a siren in the background. "All right. Do whatever the paramedics tell you and I'll be right there."

The fifteen-minute drive to the barn took me ten. When I arrived I found enough lights to fill a stadium—two police cars, racetrack security, and an ambulance all had their lights flashing.

"What's happening?" I asked.

Maggie hurried to my side and linked her arm with mine. "They couldn't revive him," she said, her voice shaky. Liz wasn't far behind, her face ashen. She was on the brink of tears. I opened my arms and she fell into them, her body trembling.

A crime scene unit set up and started taking photographs.

A security officer materialized from the shadows. "Looks like a stroke or a heart attack."

"Won't know until we have an autopsy," a policeman added.

A uniformed EMT walked up and asked the officer, "Okay if we take the body?"

A second policeman, cellphone to his ear, held up a hand.

Everyone waited.

The cop punched off, folded his phone, and returned it to his belt. "After the CSI people finish, we're sending the body to Albuquerque for an autopsy." He turned to the EMT. "You have an address for the morgue?"

The EMT nodded. "Of course."

The police moved chairs out into the hallway, away from the office. They wanted to interview Liz and Maggie. I stood behind them, a hand on each shoulder, hoping my touch would lend support.

When the questioning ended, Liz and Maggie got ready to drive back to the lodge just as the sky in the east began to lighten.

"Be careful," I said, giving them each a final hug.

The ambulance left with the body.

Police turned off their flashing lights and drove away.

"Want me to stay with you?" the racetrack security officer asked?

I shook my head. "Thanks, I'll be okay," I answered.

Alone, I watched the sunrise, stared at a cup of coffee, and thought about Gus.

No trainer. No jockey. A sick horse. The race only three days away.

What would Gus do if he were in my shoes?

CHAPTER 66

Ruidoso Downs, barn #57

Shortly after sunrise, Andrea came to see me.

"Someone needs to tell Mr. Payne." She looked scared, like she didn't want to be the one with bad news. "Will you call him?"

I dialed the number of Futurity Stables in Albuquerque and asked for Edgar Payne.

"He's not available," the receptionist replied. "May I take a message."

I told her about Gus and left my number.

Lupe, Rick, and Emily squeezed into the tiny office. I gave them my best pep talk. "Gus would want us to work harder, to try to cover for him."

With determined faces, they went about our morning routine.

Then I called Gerald McCastland in Canyon and told him what had happened.

"What can I do to help?" Mac asked.

"Would you come to Ruidoso and take over as trainer?"

He hesitated, "Jim Bob, I don't know. I've never handled horses in a big race like the All American."

"Horse, singular. I want you to call the shots for Orphan. Edgar Payne will have to decide what to do about Midnight Dash."

"Can't you could find someone more qualified."

I gave him the strongest words I could think of, words that would convey the depth of our predicament. "The race is only three days away and we have no jockey, no trainer. Can you be here this afternoon?"

After a pause of several seconds, he answered, "Okay."

Work seemed to help. Lupe and I mucked out the stalls. Rick and Emily each took a horse and prepared them for Andrea. "Mac will be here this afternoon," I said to each.

Lupe proved a rock for the others. His steadiness reassured the horses, making both Orphan and Midnight feel nothing was wrong.

Liz and Maggie came and brought sandwiches for lunch. When Mac arrived in the middle of the afternoon and started giving orders, his first decision startled me.

"I want Liz to ride Orphan for this afternoon's exercise."

"Why not have Andrea? She's been doing it every day since we lost Robert."

"You asked me to be your trainer. You want me to run this place, or you want someone else?"

"All right, but I want you to ask Liz."

He did. Liz said yes.

Mac and I went out to watch Andrea gallop Midnight, and Liz to do the same on Orphan. For the first time since the time trials,

Orphan looked perky, like his old self.

That evening Mac met with Liz and me. His words hit us like a bombshell, "Liz, I'd like you to ride Orphan in the All American," he said.

CHAPTER 67

Ruidoso Downs, Barn #57

Mac had arrived late Friday afternoon.

An hour later, he'd asked Liz to ride Orphan.

Only twelve hours later, on Saturday morning, we learned the racetrack stewards turned us down. They told us all riders must be licensed, approved jockeys to participate in a big race like the All American.

Immediately, Mac petitioned for a hearing. Arthur Reynolds, Chairman of the Board of the Ruidoso Downs Racetrack Corporation, scheduled it for two p.m. Mac asked me, as Orphan's owner, to accompany him to the meeting.

Normally, the thought of appearing before the governing body of one of the world's great racetracks would have rattled me. On Saturday, however, I didn't have time to be intimidated, or to even think about it.

Police came to re-investigate Gus' death. They tape recorded interviews with me, alone, with me and my family, and then with me and the employees. While I supported their efforts to probe the death of my friend, their approach seemed pedantic, repetitious, and a waste of time.

In the middle of all the activity, Edgar Payne arrived with his new trainer, Carlos Lopez. I tried to be civil, to cooperate. Payne, however, made demands that I thought unreasonable. It seemed impossible for the two of us to agree on anything, so I called Mac, introduced him to Carlos, and left to have lunch with Liz and Maggie at a nearby McDonald's.

We stood in line to get our food and then took a booth by the front window.

"Dad, you need to ease up," Liz said.

"Tell that to Payne," I snapped.

"What does he want?"

"He wants to take over, to run the stable." I stood. "Anyone want more catsup?" Both my daughter and my wife shook their heads. I stomped off to get more condiments.

Liz quizzed me when I returned, "He's telling you what to do with Orphan?"

"Well, no, but he wants to change everything else."

"Such as?"

"The schedule," I said. "The feeding. The exercising. The assignment of stalls. Even the location for bathing the horses."

"For Midnight Dash?"

"Yes, for his prima donna filly."

She gave me a big smile. "Why not let him?"

I put down the catsup and eased back in my seat.

Both Liz and Maggie continued eating.

The more I thought about it, the more it seemed Liz was right. I calmed down a little. "Okay," Finally, I agreed.

"It'll be hard for Edgar Payne to argue with someone who says yes all the time," Maggie added.

I thought about her comment for a few moments while I returned to my Big Mac. "So that's how you win your arguments with me?"

"Of course."

The two of them laughed. I finished my burger.

"You don't really care where he bathes his horse," Liz said. "You just resent his ordering everyone around when he does it."

I chuckled. "I refuse to answer on the grounds that—"

"On the grounds that he's a horse's ass," Liz added.

"Liz." Maggie said.

"Well, he is."

I looked at my watch—1:30.

"We'd better get back for the big meeting."

At two o'clock Mac and I entered the boardroom to find seven people. Chairman Reynolds introduced us to four board members, a representative of the jockey's association, and the racetrack starter, Anthony Sanchez. We took our places around a huge, oval conference table with high-backed, plush, conference chairs.

Reynolds called the meeting to order. "As you know, Dr. Masterson has lost both his jockey and his trainer this week, and his horse, Orphan, has apparently been poisoned. His new trainer, Mr. McCastland, is asking special dispensation to use a novice jockey in the race tomorrow."

No one spoke and I sensed a profound tension in the room. I guessed they regarded our case like a keg of dynamite—one that had to be handled carefully.

Finally, the representative of the jockey association opened the discussion, "We have dozens of fully qualified jockeys here in this area," he said, his voice soft, conciliatory. "Why not hire one of them?"

Mac raised a hand.

Chairman Reynolds nodded.

"We propose Elizabeth Masterson. She's raised Orphan since he was two weeks old. Our horse is recovering from a recent poison incident and badly needs the trust and reassurance a familiar rider would provide."

The starter, Anthony Sanchez, spoke next, his voice louder, more authoritarian, "There's a reason why we require licensed jockeys." He leaned forward, elbows on the table, his voice rising with each word, "We all know the starting procedure often determines the winner in short, quarter-mile racing. A poor start by an inexperienced jockey can determine the race's outcome, not just for the horse that falters, but also for those nearby." He paused, then in a decisive voice, one that filled the room with a commanding presence, he concluded, "The last thing we need is a foul-up that affects other horses."

I looked around the table at the stewards. Most were frowning. One nodded his head in agreement with Sanchez.

Mac raised his hand again.

Reynolds gestured.

"We agree," Mac said, "and we're willing to withdraw our horse rather than cause an accident."

Several of those at the table stirred. It was obvious that no one wanted one of the leading contenders to withdraw.

Mac continued, "I propose a trial run, a breeze, with your starter, Tony Sanchez, as the judge. We could load Orphan and two of our other horses, one on each side, into the starting gate and let Tony observe our jockey's ability to control the horse."

A hush fell over the room. No one moved.

"Tony, what do you think?" Chairman Reynolds asked.

"Okay," Sanchez answered. "Tomorrow morning, 7:30, before the track gets busy." He turned in his chair and looked straight at me. "I don't care if she is your daughter. If I get the slightest indication that she's a potential danger to the race, I won't allow her to ride."

CHAPTER 68

Sunday, the Day Before the Race, at the Starting Gate

Just as the sun peeked over the eastern foothills, we took Orphan and the two other horses out onto the track and waited near the starting gate. We called this race a breeze—everyone knew it was anything but.

Andrea rode the first horse. Mac loaded her and her mount into gate one. Liz rode Orphan. He loaded them into gate two.

A borrowed jockey, one we'd hired from a nearby stable, rode the other horse. Mac loaded them into gate three.

All three horses loaded smoothly—no kicking or bucking. Liz looked poised and confident, except for her eyes. I could see by the way her gaze darted from point to point that she was in a state of anxiety.

Mac raised a hand. "We're ready," he said.

Anthony Sanchez pushed the button. The bell rang loudly as the gates sprang open—all three horses made a clean start. Orphan took an immediate lead and never looked back, winning the breeze by a huge margin. From the starting gate, a quarter-mile away, it was difficult to tell, but I guessed it at least two lengths.

It was a performance that impressed everyone who saw it. Everyone except Tony Sanchez.

"I'll report to Chairman Reynolds," he said with a scowl. "He'll call you within the hour."

We walked the horses back to our barn where the grooms bathed and fed them.

I looked for Liz and when I found her, I held out my arms. "You were terrific," I said, holding her tightly.

"Thanks, Dad." The strength of her embrace surprised me.

"You saved our bacon this morning."

"Not me," she said as she relaxed her grasp and eased away. "That was Orphan."

"I'm trying to give you a compliment."

She reached up on tip-toes and kissed me on the forehead. "And you did, but I'm trying to tell you, it's not me. Orphan loves to run."

She left to change clothes.

We waited.

An hour went by.

Then another.

Mac got out his cellphone. "I think I'd better call Reynolds."

Just then, a white Lexus SUV pulled up in front of our barn.

"Wait," I said.

Reynolds and Sanchez strode into the barn, both looking grim.

"I thought it would be best to come and give you our decision face-to-face rather than over the phone," Reynolds said.

"We appreciate your concern," Mac replied.

"Tony?" Reynolds nodded to the starter.

"We think it would set a dangerous precedent to allow your

daughter to ride. I'm sorry, but there's good reason to use only qualified jockeys."

Mac looked down, shaking his head.

"What about the jockey who rode your other horse?" Reynolds asked. "Is he available?"

"You saw the breeze?" I asked.

"Of course," he replied. "I was in the grandstand on the owners' level with binoculars."

"You saw how Liz handled Orphan."

He nodded. "She did well, but—"

Sanchez interrupted. "We're talking about the All American. If it were any other race, it would be different."

"I think we're all looking for the same thing," I countered, "a safe race."

Both Reynolds and Sanchez nodded.

"Let's analyze this for a moment," I insisted.

Sanchez sighed, an exasperated release of breath.

I looked at my wristwatch. "I ask that you give this two more minutes. After you hear me out, I'll accept whatever decision you make."

Sanchez looked at Reynolds.

Reynolds said, "Okay, two minutes."

At that moment the jockey in barn #56 led a horse out to his walker. He was the same jockey who had ridden our third horse that morning. I pointed to him.

"There's the fellow you're suggesting I hire to ride Orphan."

Reynolds and Sanchez looked.

"I don't even know his name. I'll bet you don't either."

The two racetrack officials continued to watch him.

"For sure, our horse doesn't know him, doesn't feel any reassurance from this stranger."

Sanchez looked at his watch, obviously impatient.

"On the other hand we have Elizabeth Masterson, the person who broke the horse, who has practically lived with him for his entire life, and who you saw ride him this morning."

I paused to let my words sink in.

"We all want a safe race. I feel so strongly about this . . . I'm only going to enter Orphan in the race . . . if you allow Liz to ride him."

Reynolds and Sanchez looked shocked.

"Surely you're not going to withdraw from the All American?" Reynolds asked.

"We have a horse that's been poisoned. We've lost our trainer *and* our jockey. How often has that happened in the history of this race?"

Neither said anything for a long moment. Obviously, no one knew of a precedent.

"I think Gus was murdered," I said. "I believe someone is deliberately trying to keep us out of contention."

"If you drop out, they'll have won," Sanchez said, his voice rising.

"If you force us to use a strange jockey, you lessen our chances. You're aiding and abetting the very people who are poisoning horses and killing people."

"That's a stretch," Sanchez yelled. "We're only trying to run this race by the rules."

Reynolds raised his hand, a gesture to quiet everybody down.

"No, we're trying to do the *right* thing," he said.

"Arthur," Sanchez shouted. "No!"

The racetrack owner frowned at the starter and shook his head, then turned to me. "I think you're right. Perhaps we'll have a safer race if your daughter rides Orphan."

CHAPTER 69

Ruidoso Downs, Barn # 57

Monday. Labor Day. Race day. Beautiful calm sunrise, no wind, scattered clouds, and a temperature of forty-nine degrees. The weatherman predicted a high of seventy-eight by race time—a perfect day for the All American Futurity.

We followed our regular routine, and the morning flew by.

When it came time, Mac led Orphan out to the walker. One of the grooms placed old Nellybelle on the opposite side. Orphan looked good, relaxed, confident. Rick and Emily went to the stalls to muck out the droppings, turn over the sawdust and woodchips, fill the large blue buckets with grain, and stuff the hay nets with fresh alfalfa.

I thought about the day, the pressure to win, and how many things could go wrong. To get my mind off potential problems, I pulled out the tattered old payoff sheet, and for the hundredth time went through the numbers. I looked, one last time, at the winner's line—78 percent of a million dollars if we won. It didn't seem possible.

Race time came at twelve o'clock, noon. We heard the bugler, a guy they had flown in from Los Angeles for the occasion, give the call for the first race. Even in our barn, we felt the excitement. The ninth race was the All-American and set for 4:40 p.m.

No one from our barn went to the early races except Edgar Payne. He came by, talked with Carlos and Andrea, went to the stall where Midnight Dash was resting, looked in for a moment, and left. He made a point of ignoring me, which was fine. I certainly had nothing to say to him.

Liz, Maggie, Mac, the three grooms, and I waited. Race after race we heard the crowd noise and felt tension build. When we heard the announcement for the eighth race, Mac and Liz went to get Orphan from his stall. We were assigned number five—the position with blue colors.

Together, the seven of us walked Orphan up the hill from the stable to the racetrack. Mac led and held the lead rope. Liz carried her saddle and walked beside him, her presence in front giving reassurance. The three grooms, Lupe on one side, Rick and Emily on the other, walked abreast, also trying to lend support. Maggie and I followed.

Horses, jockeys, trainers, and grooms from the previous race, walked past us, returning to the stables. A parade of emotion.

"Good luck," someone said. "I've got five dollars riding on you."

I smiled and waved.

At the entrance to the track we parted. Liz, Lupe, and Mac went into the paddock to saddle up and be inspected. Rick and Emily headed up into the grandstand. Maggie and I found a place inside the track, near the 400-yard marker, as close as we could get to the finish line.

The announcer started his spiel about the big race. I heard my name mentioned as owner of number five.

Minutes later the horses left the paddock to parade in front of the grandstand. Liz went by on Orphan. I gave her a "thumbs up." A sense of pride welled inside as I watched her being led to the starting gate. Maggie took my hand and squeezed it. We watched them load the horses, two by two, into the gates.

Standing near the paddock, a little more than four hundred yards away, binoculars glued to my eyes, I could see Anthony Sanchez, the starter, as he pushed his button. Bells rang, doors flew open, and the ten fastest horses in America jumped out of the gate. My breathing stopped.

Orphan stumbled. Not a fall, not even a bad misstep, but enough of a fumble that I could see, looking head-on and at this distance, that Orphan came out of the gate behind all the other horses. My stomach churned as I watched over 10,000 pounds of horseflesh come thundering toward me—with Orphan in the rear. Second by second he remained in the middle of the track, shut off by two horses in front of him. As they came closer, approaching the 220-yard marker, I lowered the binoculars and watched with my naked eyes.

Then, the two horses directly in the middle parted, and a horse leaped through the opening with a sudden burst of speed. In the next five seconds they shot past me, and though I couldn't be sure, it seemed the nose of the horse in the lead wore blue blinkers.

The next few seconds ticked off in slow motion as I realized how poorly I had chosen my position to watch the race. The crowd roared, and all I could see was the rear end of ten horses in a cloud of dust—no way to tell who had won.

My lungs started breathing again, and I looked around, anxiously searching for reaction. "Who won?" I yelled, directing my question to anyone within hearing distance.

"Photo," someone answered.

"A photo finish," Maggie said as she pointed to the big scoreboard just west of the winner's circle.

The next forty-five seconds seemed like hours. A hush fell over the grandstand as twenty thousand people waited for the officials to publish the winners on the scoreboard.

Then, a cheer went up, and I scanned the big board to find the numbers five, seven, and one.

Horse number one came in third, horse number seven was second. Horse number five had won the race.

Orphan's number was five.

My horse—my daughter—had won the All American Futurity.

CHAPTER 70

The Winners Circle, Ruidoso Downs

Maggie hugged me.

Dazed, heart pounding, palms sweating, I hugged her back.

We kissed. We danced a little jig. It seemed too good to be true.

"Let's go congratulate our jockey," I said.

Maggie kissed me again. "Yes, let's."

We tried, but the crowd was so thick it didn't seem possible we'd ever make it to the Winner's Circle. Little by little we pushed our way forward. Ahead we could see Mac leading Orphan from the track, Liz still in the saddle.

Liz waved. Then she leaned down to speak with a uniformed security guard, and pointed in our direction.

We kept trying to work our way through the crowd until, suddenly, people parted and two security guards appeared.

"You the owners?" one of the guards asked.

Maggie nodded. "Oh yes." she shouted.

We had it made. The guards escorted us into the Winner's Circle where we found Mac and Lupe holding on tight to the halter, no doubt remembering what had happened the last time, when camera flashes spooked Orphan.

Arthur Reynolds joined us in the circle with a huge piece of cardboard. A public relations team arranged us around the horse—Mac and Lupe on one side, Reynolds, Maggie and me on the other. Liz sat in the saddle with a bouquet of red roses spilling across her arms. Reynolds held his cardboard by one corner, Mac held the other. It was about five feet long and two feet wide.

At first I thought it would be a sign, "The Winner," or "All American," or something about the racetrack. It wasn't. It was a huge photo enlargement of a check in the amount of one million dollars. Someone had taken a black magic marker and written my name on the payee line.

More photographs. Blinding flashes of light. Thirty seconds of furious activity.

Then, as fast as the crowd had mushroomed into a frenzy, it dissipated. The photographers moved on, people left to collect their winnings, and the horses for the last race of the day paraded the track on their way to the starting gates.

Arthur Reynolds congratulated us and walked toward the tunnel.

Liz slipped down out of the saddle to walk with us.

Lupe took Orphan's reins and led him toward the path to the stable.

A large, angry man blocked his way—Edgar Payne.

Payne's face held a menacing scowl and he carried a two-by-four, a rough piece of wood about three feet long. I'd seen that look before—twice. Once in the hallway outside the Potter County Courtroom, and again after the Sheriff's Sale when Paul Edwards had outbid him. Only this time Payne's eyes blazed with maniacal craziness, a distorted mask that signaled a break with reality.

"You bastard," he yelled at the horse. "If it hadn't been for you I'd have won."

Lupe froze. He didn't know what to do, what to expect.

I did—but too late.

Payne swung the two-by-four and struck Orphan's left front leg. The blow hit just below the knee with a sickening crack.

A split-second later I tackled Payne and knocked him to the ground.

Orphan fell in a whinny of pain.

"He's got a gun." someone yelled.

I rolled over, landing on Payne's right arm, the weight of my body pinning his gun hand to the ground. I felt him pulling, struggling to release his arm. I grabbed his thumb, jerked with all my might, and felt it snap.

His arm and the gun came out from under me, Payne screaming in agony. The gun went off.

I felt a splatter of warm liquid hit my face.

CHAPTER 71

Ruidoso Downs

Police pronounced Edgar Payne "dead at the scene," the single bullet from his gun striking him in the temple, killing him instantly and spattering me with his blood. Police took statements from dozens of witnesses. All confirmed he died of his own hand. No one blamed me.

The vets from the orthopedic center came for Orphan. They gave him a shot to put him out of his pain, loaded him into a truck—what they called their Equine Ambulance—and took him for treatment.

They cancelled the next race, race #10, the last race of the day.

I thought it ironic that—in the incident which triggered Edgar Payne's anger—his horse, Midnight Dash, had placed second in the All American, only a fraction of an inch behind Orphan. It should have been a cause for celebration. All the owners I know would have been elated to come that close to winning.

But not Payne.

He was crazy, and at the end his temper did him in.

I went to the orthopedic vets where I found both good news and bad. The good news was that Orphan would not have to be put down. The bad—he would never be able to race again.

The next day, Robert, Orphan's former jockey, was questioned about Payne and his trainer. Robert admitted he was a cocaine user and told police he'd been getting his drugs from Carlos Lopez. Payne knew this and threatened to expose Robert—which would have caused the Jockey's Association to revoke his license—unless Robert fed Orphan moldy hay and poisoned his water.

Robert also said he heard Payne offer Carlos Lopez $100,000 if he would slip the little white pills into Gus' drinking water. At first Lopez refused, said he didn't want the money, but Payne knew old secrets Lopez thought lost in Mexico. He had evidence that Lopez had killed Anna Garcia. Payne threatened exposure unless Lopez agreed to administer the pills.

The pills were only supposed to make Gus ill, but Lopez used too many, and they turned lethal. Police filed charges.

I went to see Robert, to thank him for coming forward with his testimony. We had a heart-to-heart talk about his drug problem. I offered to pay for treatment at a clinic in Phoenix. He accepted.

The next few days dragged by as we wound up loose ends. The racetrack asked me to stop by for the winner's purse. I picked up our checks—$100,000 for Mac, $100,000 for Liz, $10,000 for Lupe, and checks of $5,000 each for Rick and Emily.

As expected, they had a big one for me—$780,000.

Then I immediately wrote a personal check for $100,000 to Mrs. Gus Gonzalez and mailed it, my heart more than saddened that Gus couldn't share our joy.

We purchased a spiffy new horse trailer for Orphan.

HARRY HAINES

By the end of the week we were able to load our horse, broken leg now in a cast, and head back home to Texas.

CHAPTER 72

Late October, Carnegie Hall, New York City

Promoters hyped the recital as "The Three Sopranos." Tickets sold out in record time, but Liz reserved box seats for Maggie, her grandmother, and me—her family.

In the last few minutes before they dimmed the lights, I thumbed through the program. Roberta Fancher had two pages, a big glamorous photograph, and paragraph after paragraph of biographical info about her career.

Next came a similar presentation for Suzanne Griggs. The photo and bio followed the same format—impressive information about another of the world's greatest singers. The writer added an interesting paragraph about Griggs's early years in Lubbock, Texas.

When I came to the write-up for Elizabeth Masterson, I laughed. The photograph showed her in the Winner's Circle at the All American Futurity, riding togs and all. When my mother-in-law saw the photo, she went into apoplexy. "My God, they've ruined her. Everyone will think Liz is nothing but a cowgirl."

Maggie fanned her mother.

I read on to find the biographical information described Liz's battle with leukemia and a short narrative about GvHD. It ended with the statement that, "She is now in permanent remission."

The lights dimmed and Roberta Fancher walked on stage to thunderous applause. She sang "Ah. Je veux vivre" from Gounod's *Romeo and Juliet*. It was beautiful.

Suzanne Griggs followed with "Romance" by Berlioz, from *The Damnation of Faust*. As expected, it too was a stunning performance.

Then came Elizabeth Masterson, the tiny singer from Bushland, Texas, who was so small she could substitute as a jockey. She sang "Un bel di," her signature aria from Puccini's *Madam Butterfly*. When she finished she looked over at us and smiled—the same, big, toothy grin I had seen when she was seated in a saddle at the end of the Labor Day race.

The entire audience leapt to their feet, clapping and cheering—something I'd never witnessed before. A standing ovation for the first number.

Maggie squeezed my hand, pulling me to her. Our lips touched. Then we stood and, like everyone else in the hall, clapped for our daughter.

CREDITS

A published novel is rarely the result of a single person's labor. And that is certainly the case for this one.

Doris Wenzel, my editor, comes first in line among the dozens who helped make this story a reality. She chose it for Mayhaven's "Award for Fiction" and then became the major referee in decisions about final editing.

Andrea Brown, my agent, had the original idea for the setting, the characters, and eventually, the story. She has guided my fiction writing and, especially through the Big Sur Writers Workshops, has been my mentor.

Paula Silici, the lady with the blue pencil, went through the manuscript and made hundreds of suggestions. Paula has the unique ability to criticize and the same time make you think it's a compliment.

The technical details in this book were checked by Sharon Nelson (an oncology R.N.) and Jo Walker (who owns and races quarter horses). Thanks, Sharon and Jo; I couldn't have done the book without your expertise.

The two biggest influences on my fiction writing have been the Iowa Summer Writing Festival and the Maui Writers Retreat and Conference. I went to Iowa four times and took their advanced novel classes with Mary Helen Stefoniak, Sands Hall, Jonas Agee, and Susan Chehawk. At Maui, Bob Mayer and William Martin were my instructors for the two summers I attended. When it comes to point of view, character motivation, or any of the thousands of technical tidbits writers must master to write a publishable story, I have to say I learned it from these great teachers—magnified by the unique settings at Iowa and Maui.

Every writer needs a critique group and I've been lucky to have two that worked on this novel. Janda Raker, Joan Sikes, Diane Neal, Jarrod Neal, and Robert Gross met at the church for about three hours every Thursday afternoon and read aloud. I learned from hearing both their manuscripts and mine—we all gained from the exchange of ideas. Wednesdays at noon I joined Betty Decker, Bettie Haller, Scott Williams, and Jodi Thomas for lunch and the trading of criticism; the focus was always, "How we could make our stories better."

And finally a word about motivation for writing. Fred Harris—former US Senator from Oklahoma, now retired, living in Albuquerque, and writing novels—told me he thinks the two most boring human activities are studying and writing. I agree with Fred, writing is boring and requires powerful stimulus to get it done. I've found that I do it best in a restaurant, early in the morning, sitting alone in a booth, with white noise to block out aural distractions and the pleasant aroma of food to create a comfort zone.

For *Orphan*, I learned that Denny's Restaurant on I-40 in Amarillo was the ideal spot. Manager Bruce Wilson always welcomed me and never charged me rent (even though I sometimes sat in that booth for four or five hours). But the real secret to writing is, in my humble opinion, caffeine. And it is to Diane McGinnis, the world's best waitress, who provided me with at least 1,000 cups of coffee, that this book is here for you to read.